THE ONLY GAME IN TOWN

THE ONLY
GAME IN TOWN

CHARLES EINSTEIN

CUTTING EDGE

ISBN-13: 978-1-962896-74-0

Published by
Cutting Edge Books
PO Box 8212
Calabasas, CA 91372
www.cuttingedgebooks.com

THE COUNT

CHAPTER ONE
NOTHING AND NOTHING

WHEN THE WASHINGTON SHORTSTOP took the soft lob throw, the runner from first was almost upon him, and the shortstop did not have time to step out to his left to get out of the way of the slide. He went up in the air instead to get the throw to first base for the double play, and at that moment four big bertha cameras on the photographers' ledge that lipped the mezzanine structure on the first base side at Yankee Stadium—all four, together, snapped him, frozen in the air.

Also in the mezzanine, back of home plate, a man threw the switch that would change the picture on the television screen, so that now what the viewers saw was a close-up of the play at first base. Through the expert abilities of this man and of his cameramen, through the spectacular scientific achievement of television itself, through the beneficence of the sponsor and the benediction of the Yankees, the picture flashed through the air and onto television screens as far north as the small upstate city of Conway, New York.

Walt Corio, sitting in a bar there, watched without really watching as the shortstop went up and over the runner to make his throw. Corio knew something about baseball. He was thrown out of organized ball in 1946. His name was not Corio then. His name was Carsi. You may remember him.

Carsi and four others were barred from baseball for life. They were teammates on a ball club in a minor league in Texas. They did not conspire with gamblers. That is, they did not bag games for somebody else. They did have other people place their money for them while they themselves bet on the outcomes of the games in which they played. This way, it took longer for them to be caught.

Carsi changed his name to Corio when it happened, and left that part of the country, and eventually he got a job with a company that made gears in Herkimer, New York. There he played with the company ball team, and after a time he found out that the production supervisor at the factory knew how to put in a good word with a man named Kelly, who was general manager of the Conway Bears, a minor-league ball club upstate.

That way Walt Corio returned to baseball.

He had the heart of a gambler, Walt Corio did, and he came back carefully. He was a man for whom self-protection had become a necessity in life. His return to organized ball was predicated not on a desire to play, nor as an illegal, perhaps explosively dramatic means of wiping out past sins (though he was the kind of man who felt, along with many an honest baseball man and fan, that something like the Black Sox scandal should not erase the accomplishments of someone like Shoeless Joe Jackson from the record book for all time). No, and he did not return to baseball with the idea that he might start, once again, betting against himself.

None of these possibilities could be excluded completely, but they were not behind what he did. The reason was, basically and simply, that playing baseball was an easier—to be sure, even a more enjoyable—way for someone like Walt Corio to earn a salary than working on a factory production line.

It was three o'clock in the afternoon when he got off the bus from Herkimer and had his first look at Conway, New York. He neither liked nor disliked what he saw. He crossed the street from the bus station and went into a saloon that had a neon beer ad in the window and a large stained shingle over the door that said *Olde Tavern*. Inside, there was a television set on a shelf at the end of the bar nearest the door. There was a ball game on, and Corio went far enough down along the bar so he could see without turning his head too much. It was the Yankees playing Washington. Taped against a mirror in the center of the bar was a thin, lightweight black slate—a scoreboard. The names of the teams on the slate were BEARS and BOSTON, and across the inning spaces it said, spelled out in dim chalk, NITE.

There were only two people in the place when Corio got there—the bartender, and a girl, sitting by herself at the bar, drinking beer. Corio sat himself two stools away from the girl and ordered a beer. When the bartender came and stopped in front of him, Corio said he wanted a beer and pointed at the scoreboard. "You keep that thing up?"

"All the time," the bartender said. "Did you want Miller's?"

"All right," Corio said. "This a good baseball town?"

"Fair," the bartender said. He reached a bottle out of the cooler. "Population for population, we're a better baseball town than Albany. 'Course, it's hard to compare."

"Owned by Philadelphia?"

"Outright," the bartender said. "Now *those* Bears, this town's got an interest in them. Surprise you, the way people want to know what Philadelphia did. You like baseball?"

"Some."

"You look like a ballplayer," the bartender said. "Don't he, Jo Ann?"

The girl looked at Corio. "He does," she said, "at that." She seemed, to Corio's swift and not altogether amateur appraisal, to be both uncommonly pretty and uncommonly leggy; she had black hair, and despite her obvious youth her face, while not a hard face, was an expert one, as if surely it was not the face she wore upon arising in the morning.

"Ever play ball?" she said.

"A little."

"Like to play here?"

"Might."

"This club in town has room for a man," the girl said, still looking at him.

Corio noticed immediately that she had used the word *club*— not, as ninety-nine women out of a hundred would say, *team*. He thought for a moment, and then he said, "Maybe I'll drop in on them."

"Well," the girl said, and smiled at the bartender. "Archie, what do you know?"

"Don't ask me," Archie the bartender said. "I don't know nothing." He looked over at Corio. "You want to know anything about the Conway Beats, ask her. She's the town's number one—"

"Fan," the girl said. "Wasn't that what you were going to say, Archie?"

"Exactly," the bartender said. "Tell him about young Joe Whittier."

"Archie," the girl said.

Archie shrugged. "He's going to—What'd you say your name was?"

"Walt," Corio said.

"Walt's going to find out anyway," Archie said. "Plays second base for Stat Hunter, Joe does."

"Hunter's the manager. He was in the big league." The way Corio said it, it was both a statement and an inquiry.

"You're damn right he was in the big league," Archie said. "Be there yet if he could throw a ball. He makes one good throw and his arm kills him for a week."

"What's he doing here?"

"What am *I* doing here?" the bartender said. "You make the dollar. What do you want?"

Corio fingered the rim of his glass. "I mean, you'd think he could have a job somewhere else, higher up, maybe still in the big league. A coach or something."

Archie said, "Who the hell knows? This Hunter's crazier than most. A nice guy. A *nice guy*. You ask anybody, they'll tell you what a nice guy Stat Hunter is. But you want to know something, all he knows how to do is play ball. They tell him he's through in the big leagues, he looks around. Philadelphia tells him go ahead, you can play ball, play for the Conway team we got in Class C. While you're at it, manage the bas—" Archie became aware of the girl sitting there—"manage them too. Nobody else'll manage them. We'll pay you double. Maybe we'll bring you up again and you can play for us. What the hell."

"Sure," Walt Corio said. "Will you and the lady have a beer with me?"

The bartender nodded approval of this thought and put his arm down in the cooler again. There was a heightening of sound from the television set in the front corner, and they looked and saw Berra of the Yankees on his way around third, getting a hummingbird thrust of a handshake from Crosetti, the third-base coach, as he came around.

Archie the bartender said, "Home run."

"He hits the long ball," Corio said.

"He don't usually get them off that pitcher."

"You sound," Corio said, "like you know a lot about baseball."

The girl, Jo Ann, said, "He likes to sound that way." She smiled at Corio. It was almost a thoughtful smile. "He's got a wife, too."

"She's talking about Stat Hunter," the bartender said.

Jo Ann nodded. "Divorced him two years ago. That's why he came here. He came to Conway to forget."

"Well," Corio said, "from a quick look at the town, I'd say he made a fine choice."

Archie the bartender drank some beer. He was a little man whose face bore a look of constant surprise. It was a pale face, and the Adam's apple was overlarge. "Anyway," he said, "there's Hunter and Joe Whittier and that's the whole ball club."

The girl, Jo Ann, said, "Never mind about Whittier."

"What do you mean, never mind about Whittier?" Archie grinned at Corio. "She's soft on Whittier. Soft on ballplayers generally, if you ask me. Had a yen for Stat Hunter till she met up with Whittier, but—"

"Archie," the girl said.

"Well, all right," the bartender said. "Whittier. Plays second base. A heller, that boy, a real heller. Headed for the big leagues if I ever saw it. Does everything. On the field and off it, too. Ooh! Drinks, gambles …" Archie paused and looked significantly at Jo Ann. Then he went on. "Owes half the town. That boy's in debt, Walt. Can't be more than twenty, twenty-one year old and he's in debt right up to his jawbone. The only thing's going to save him, if he gets a call to the majors, gets some more of that baseball money. Save him and save Stat Hunter too. That's the only way a manager can produce with a bush-league club like this one. The hell with winning the pennant. You got to come up with a player, is all."

Archie consumed some more beer. "Don't smoke, though. Never seen young Joe Whittier with a cigarette in his hand."

Corio set down his glass. "How come Hunter puts up with all that?"

"Who said Hunter knew about it? This is only Hunter's first year, and it's still only June yet. Besides, it ain't known all over."

Corio looked at Jo Ann. "No?"

She looked back at him. "No."

"Gambles, you say," Corio said.

"You ought to see him go," Archie said.

"Me," Corio said offhandedly, "I can take a little action too. You wouldn't know of something?"

The bartender and Jo Ann looked at each other. Then Archie said, "The house takes it. It's fair, but you play the house. Isn't that right, Jo Ann?"

"Yup," she said.

"It's the Black Widow," Archie said. "Out on Route 47, west of town, maybe two mile. You don't figure on missing it."

"Okay."

"Don't get there much ahead of ten o'clock," Archie said, "and tell the waiter you want to see somebody downstairs."

Jo Ann said, "Maybe he's just kidding."

"I'm not kidding," Corio said.

"About the ballplayer part," she said.

"No," he said. "Matter of fact, I figure to be up at the club offices this afternoon. Talk to a man named Kelly there."

"Well," Jo Ann said, "I might see you there."

"You?"

"Mind?"

"No."

"It's like Archie says," the girl said to Corio. "I like ballplayers."

"Like Whittier and Hunter," Archie said, "is what she means, Walt. Funny thing is, they don't get along so hot."

"Whittier and Hunter?"

"Oh, it ain't out in the open," Archie said. "The kid showboats a little too much and the old man don't like it."

"Well, it works both ways," Corio said. "Maybe the kid's got a right to showboat."

"Maybe," Jo Ann said. She looked steadily at Corio. "I'd like to hear some more of your opinions some day."

Corio set down his glass. "Any time."

"It's a date," Jo Ann said. "And thank you for the beer."

When Corio got outside he stopped momentarily. A sign down the street said *Hotel,* and he headed that way. The hotel was not large, but it had a sitting-room off the lobby, and Corio went in there and took a piece of hotel stationery from the rack at the little desk, and sat down and wrote:

> *Steve old Buddy,*
> *Find out everything there is to find out about a woman named Marian Hunter that was married to Stat Hunter the ballplayer. The more you find out the better and maybe we both pull it in. Write to me personal care of CONWAY BEARS CONWAY NY.*
>
> *Remember the Alamo,*
> *Walt*

Corio put a dime in the stamp machine, pulled out three 3's, stamped the letter, mailed it in the box next to the registration desk in the lobby, and smiled at the clerk. "Where's the Bank Building?"

"One block up and one block to your right," the clerk said, "sir."

"Thank you," Corio said, "sir." He went out again, walked to the Bank Building, and found that the offices of the Conway Bears were on the second floor. He walked up.

What Walt Corio knew about the man they called Stat Hunter was not much. He knew that Hunter, in the major leagues, had been as good a ballplayer as most, and had lasted longer. He knew, from reading a line about it in the paper somewhere, that Hunter, the last year or the year before, had been divorced, that it had been in the west somewhere, that the name of Hunter's wife was Marian. Walt Corio had a ballplayer's eye for pitching and a blackmailer's eye for detail. As frequently as not, he grounded out either way, but he was always prepared to take his cut.

The sign on the glass door at the head of the stairs said *Conway Bears.* Corio went in and found himself in one large office with two desks along the same wall. One of the desks, the nearest one, was unoccupied. At the other sat a lean, ulcerous-looking man who could have been, from the looks of him, almost anything—a druggist, or a railroad conductor, or a banker, or a professional dice player, or general manager of the Conway Bears in the Class C Empire League.

"Mr. Kelly?"

Lester Kelly looked up.

"I'm Corio," Walt Corio said.

"Oh," Lester Kelly said. He was the kind of man who seldom offered to shake hands, but still did not make a visitor feel unwelcome. "The ballplayer."

Walt Corio closed the door behind him. "Mr. Baumer said to see you today, about this time."

Kelly swung in his chair and put his hands back of his neck. He did not ask the other man to sit down. "He said you played some first base for him."

"And some other places," Corio said.

"What other places?"

"Around. Down south."

"Have trouble?"

"Some."

"Been in jail?"

"No."

"Well," Kelly said, "all you're asking for is a try, and that's all you're getting, so the hell with it. I can put you on for a week or so. I'm under my player limit, and we'll let Stat Hunter take a look at you. You know Hunter?"

Corio hesitated a moment. Then he said, "No. No, I don't think so. He's the manager, isn't he?"

Kelly nodded. "You married?"

"No, sir." Corio's voice was soft, and it had, faintly, the flavor of the Southwest.

"But you played in organized ball."

"It was like I said. Drifted out. You know how it is."

The man named Kelly did not indicate one way or the other whether he knew how it was. Instead, he looked away and said, "Well, Marcus'll be in town tomorrow or the next day. You know who Marcus is?"

Corio knew who Marcus was. What he said was, "No, I don't believe I do."

"Scout for the Bears," Kelly said. "The Philadelphia Bears. They own this club here. Way they're going, they might be able to use a man." Kelly reflected for a moment. "Hell, the way they're going they might be able to use me."

Corio smiled.

"All right," Lester Kelly said. "About money. I can let you have forty or fifty now. You staying at the hotel?"

"I haven't checked in any place yet."

"Well," Kelly said, "there's a tourist house where one of our players stays now. His name's Joe Whittier. New York boy originally. He's the best ballplayer we've got. Not that it makes any difference to you. You can stay with him if you want. The club will pay your room and board and I'll give you half a hundred now and that's the deal. As I say, we're under our limit. If Hunter likes you, we'll talk contract."

"That sounds fair."

Lester Kelly said, "Ah, the devil himself," and Corio looked behind him and saw the door had opened. An athletic-looking young man stood there, a young man with a prominent jaw and a crew haircut. He was not alone. There was a girl with him, and the girl was Jo Ann, the one who had been in the bar. Standing there, she was tall and black-haired. She looked directly at Corio, and her eyes had both a deep and a warning expression. *So,* Corio said to himself, *this is supposed to be the first time we've met.* It was an element that intrigued him, even as the girl intrigued him.

"Joe Whittier," Kelly said, by way of introduction. "Second base. Walt Corio. New man."

Corio and Whittier shook hands, and the younger man said, "What do you play?"

"Anywhere," Corio said, and smiled at the girl.

"This is Jo Ann," Whittier said, as if that explained it.

"Hello," she said.

"Hello, Jo Ann," Corio said. He looked at her somewhat longer than was necessary. "I'm rooming with you." He said this to Whittier, but his eyes did not leave the girl until he had completed the sentence.

"All right," Whittier said. "Les, I need some money."

Kelly turned back to his desk. "You wait till Monday like I told you."

"I can use fifteen dollars now," Whittier said.

"I told you Hunter's going to find out about that," Kelly said. "What with Marcus coming to town in a day or so you got no right doing that with your money."

"It's my money," the second baseman said.

"How long you think you can keep this up?" Kelly said. "You think Hunter's not going to find out about it?"

"What if he does? I'm leading his league, ain't I? I ain't doing him any harm, playing ball for him. What do you want?"

"Well, leave me out of it, is all," Kelly said. "I don't want to hear any more about it."

"What's fifteen dollars?"

"It's nothing," Kelly said. "Nothing for me and nothing for you and nothing for the Black Widow."

Walt Corio said, almost idly, "What's the Black Widow?"

"Gambling house," Kelly said shortly. He was looking at Joe Whittier.

"Well," Walt Corio said, and licked his lips for a moment. "Well, I think I'd better be getting along. What was the address of that rooming place? What's the name of the ball park here?"

Lester Kelly told him, and Corio shook hands all around, and departed.

Fairchild Park, home of the Conway Bears, was situated along the main-line tracks of the Delaware and Hudson Railroad a mile or so south of the Conway depot. Nobody knows how many young boys, yearning to become professional ballplayers, have gazed out of the windows of D & H trains, viewed Fairchild Park, and decided then and there upon medicine, plumbing, or the law. The site of the park, which was named for Leland Fairchild, United States senator from Conway 1892—98, was used, a good number of years ago, as a coaling station for the D & H. In time, the coaling station was moved some three city blocks north, leaving enough uncontested acreage for the construction of a ball field. Thus Fairchild Park grew up without a glorious past, a rosy future, or, for that matter, a discernible present. In common with many other sooty, ramshackle, and splinter-fenced ball yards in towns across the country, it rapidly took on that not wholly describable quality of appearing vacant and discarded even when in use.

The grandstand, which had these many years withstood the unwritten law that all minor-league ball parks at one time or another burn down, was uncovered and could, conceivably, seat nearly four thousand fans. The stands, which biennially were painted a hideous and fast-decaying green, were fronted by a sagging wire screen some thirty-five feet back of home plate; underneath on the first-base side was a long wooden hutch which served as dressing quarters for the contestants; and, starting where the stands ended shortly beyond first and third bases, a seven-foot wooden fence—also painted green, but only in election years—circled the field.

The trains ran on an embankment back of the fence from right to center field, and it was possible to see over the fence from the windows of passing railroad cars. But these days the Conway Bears played only at night, and the lighting system was such that the free view was hardly worth it.

Still, it was a way of life for the fifteen men—four infielders, one utility man, five pitchers, two catchers, and three outfielders—who made up the roster of the Conway Bears of the Class C Empire League. As human beings went, they were no less ambitious, articulate, bigoted, or clannish than the men who worked in the railroad yards up the street; nor noticeably more so. Some of them, the young ones, still were uncertain of their craft; others, the old-timers, who had been up for a trial with the majors or the fast minors, now went through the motions with the mechanical imperfection of an unaccomplished physician treating the free patients at a clinic.

One of them—his name was Andrew Hunter—had spent sixteen years in the major leagues. Now he managed the Bears and played center field for them. He was a good hitter, though he seldom hit the long ball, and his legs were all right even as he neared his thirty-seventh birthday. It was the arm that had gone on him. In consequence, he had accepted almost gratefully the opportunity to manage the Conway Bears in behalf of the Philadelphia Bears, the major-league team whose farm system, cut to the bone because of the financial inroads made by television, consisted now of just six teams, only one of them—Conway—classified as low as Class C.

All six teams in the Philadelphia farm system were called the Bears, a handy system that effected a considerable saving in home uniforms. By the time the uniforms filtered down as far as Conway, their residual advantages were negligible, but this was the least of the local worries. Next year there might be no baseball at all in Conway, and for Stat Hunter—he had earned the nickname "Stat," short for "Statutory," from rival bench jockeys at the very start of his big-league career after having had several dates with the seventeen-year-old daughter of an umpire—for Stat Hunter, at any rate, there might next year be nothing but memories and the hope of finding another baseball job somewhere. That was why it was important to him to do a workmanlike job as manager of the Bears in Conway. It was incumbent upon him to develop at least one good young player, as well as to win enough games to stay the Conway Bears from utter bankruptcy, though nowadays bankruptcy seemed inevitable for bush-league clubs, and Philadelphia was interested first of all in Joe Whittier, the coming star. All this Hunter knew.

"Ol' Stat heah," George Crimeau, the first-string catcher for the Bears, would say upon occasion, "he goin' be back in th' *big* league one of these days not too far from now, managin' one of them *ball* clubs. You listen to ol' George when he tells you about ol' Stat. Ol' George and ol' Stat used to *play* together up in th' *big* league. I know ol' Stat from way back."

In actuality, ol' George had never advanced beyond a season and a half with Syracuse of the International League, but Stat Hunter never challenged his catcher's reminiscence. Were it not for the record book, Stat Hunter could easily have come to be persuaded that he and George did indeed play in the majors together at one time or another. A ballplayer—a ballplayer who cares for his job—remembers what happened. He remembers the enemy baserunner he doubled off first after a belly catch in right-center field, and the pitcher who threw a waster too close so he hit it down the left-field line for a double, and the umpire who blew the call when he had the plate with his foot ahead of the tag. He remembers games rather than years, and innings rather than games, and situations rather than innings, and individual moments best of all. And his remembrance of associated subjects is not nearly so keen, so that if a catcher like George Crimeau said he played with you, well, by God, maybe he did. You didn't really remember him *not* playing with you, and besides, a man like George Crimeau was fortified with song and fable.

"Ol' Stat and I was playing for Chicago—when was that, Stat, you recollect? Back in 'thirty-*six*, I think it was, and ol' Magerkurth was umpirin', and *Jurges* was playin' short—you remember that now, Stat? That real *hot* day in St. Louis? Well, Paul Dean's pitchin' for *them* ..."

"I remember it," Andrew Hunter would say. "Vaguely."

Not everyone on the team exhibited Hunter's brand of patience. "You son of a bitch," Monk Gladstone, the third baseman, said one day to George Crimeau, "the closest you ever got to St. Louis was a Memorial Day double header in Peoria. I was playing for Davenport. You give it to me coming into third. I remember you real good."

"Sure," the catcher replied acquiescently. "I remember *you*. You was playin' for Davenport and I was on th' way *up*. Next season, ol' Stat and I was playin' together for *Chicago*. That's th' way it was, ain't it, Stat?"

Later, Andrew Hunter would take someone like Gladstone to one side and say, "Come on, now, Monk, leave George alone. Lay off him."

"Well, he boils my crabs," Gladstone would reply. "He never got up in the big league and he knows it."

"He's not harming anybody," the manager would say.

"I'm going to tell you something, Stat, a guy like that browns me off. I'm the ballplayer he is any day in the week and two times on holidays, and I don't go around claiming I was in the big league."

"All right," Hunter would say. "All right, Monk, all right. The hell with it."

They were little antagonisms, but over a summer of hot, sticky nights, of dismal bus rides from town to town, of second-class food and third-class hotels, they would build their own angry pyramids. Andrew Hunter knew what he was doing when he decided to set no fixed time for the players to show up before a game. That way, only the youngsters were likely to appear much ahead of practice time. The old ones, like George Crimeau and Monk Gladstone and Vagrancy Williams, the pitcher, would take their time, and there would be that much less chance for them to be sitting around together, nursing their petty hurts and irritations.

No night was a typical night in the Empire League, and yet every night was the same. No ballplayer was a typical ballplayer, and yet they too were all alike. Good nights were the nights you won, bad nights were the nights you lost, and when you were the manager you played the games all over again when you got home—the winning games as well as the losing games. If you worried only about the losing games, you were not a good manager.

In a way, you did more thinking in Class C than the managers did in the big league. You worried about the other team stealing your signals, not, as in the majors, because signal-stealing was an art, but because of necessity your signals were so simple. You had to be sure not to pitch Bo Walsh, the lefthander, on a night when Cross-Eyed. Collins, the umpire, was scheduled to work balls and strikes. You would not use Phil Gold, your second catcher, as a pinch-hitter in an early inning unless you absolutely had to, because then you could not use him to pinch-hit later on in the game, and besides, you wanted to have him to warm up your relief pitchers and to be ready to spell George Crimeau in case ol' George came down suddenly with that mysteriously private ailment which he called "th' heats," an affliction that occurred in greatest frequency late in the game when it seemed unlikely ol' George would get another turn at bat.

There was always something. This was only the first season as manager of the Bears for Andrew Hunter, but now, as early as the month of June, he felt he had become a somewhat unrealistic combination of tutor, teammate, and turnkey—not to mention his role as camp counselor, seeing to it that the youngsters wrote home twice a week.

June can be hot in Conway. The city lies in the lake valley, a valley some eight miles in width between twin ridges of the Adirondacks, and in the summer sun it becomes becalmed. Someone had put a small electric fan up on the wall of the Bears' clubhouse, and tonight, when Hunter got there, the fan was whining angrily.

Old Jack Merced, who served as caretaker for Fairchild Park and took tickets at the gate, came in the room behind him and said, "Hey, Stat, we gonna win tonight?"

"Try," Hunter said.

"That scout's coming in town tomorrow or the next day," Merced said. "What's his name? Marcus or something? Gonna have to see young Joe Whittier in action."

"That's right," Hunter said. "His name's Marcus." The manager was undressing at his locker. When he was down to his shorts, he took a safety razor down off the locker shelf, together with a tube of brushless shaving cream, and walked through the door to the combination shower and lavatory room that connected to both the home and visiting clubhouses.

Merced followed him. The two of them made up an uncommon picture—the one in front tall and black-haired, his body perhaps too slender, his face not handsome but pronounced, the eyes deep and alive, the nose and chin a trifle outsize; and the man behind, dressed in old Army pants and open-collared white shirt, whitehaired, wizened, and small of stature. Old Jack Merced's face was set in a perpetual smart, like that of a man who has applied an overdose of after-shave lotion.

"There was a letter for you, Stat. You get it?"

Hunter shook his head, looking into the mirror.

"I left it in the box," the old man said.

"Didn't look in the box."

"I'll get it for you now." Merced went out of the room. Andrew Hunter debated calling after him, to tell him to hold the letter till he got back to his locker, but it was too hot to shout. Besides, the old man was back immediately. Hunter wiped his hand on his shorts and took the letter, and when he saw who had written it, he went back into the other room with the soap still on his face and sat down on the bench in front of his locker and read the letter there.

> *Dear Daddy,*
> *We went and saw the cows, and I held open the gate they went into. Mommy said I could have a surprise. Not a kitten or a dog but a real live ...... GUESS?? The kids next door have the chiken pox. I am fine.*
>
> *x x x x x x x x*
>
> *x x x*
>
> *JANET*

Sitting there, reading the letter with the soap on his face, Andrew Hunter looked not unlike an old-time circus clown between acts. Outside the window, a window that looked out on the underside of the grandstand where it sloped down toward the field past the roof of the clubhouse, he could hear the sound of small boys running on the planking of the stands. The gate would be open now, but there still remained two hours before game time, and the only fans that would be coming this early would be the small boys.

But the sound from the window was a distant sound. Sitting there alone, Stat Hunter found his mind, like an old, old man's, retracing the past. The past was a pyramid. It built itself into the day that Marian, his wife, took their daughter and left him, and from there it sloped down and away, at an angle so steep that a man must stumble and fall.

"You're not a father," she had said. "You're a center fielder."

It was a line a comedian might have worked to get a laugh, but it was not funny. When he came home at night, he brought the game of baseball with him, and there was nothing else for him to see or know.

"You're a stranger in your own house," Marian had said to him.

He looked at her, still without seeing. "Let me alone. Lay off me for a while."

"No," she said, and he saw then that she was crying. "I'm not going to do it any more. There's not going to be any more."

He had nodded, silently. She had said this before.

But this time she went away and did not come back to him.

He had seen once, long, long ago, that she was beautiful-beautiful to him: small, and brown-haired, and made up of a soft fire that he could not describe and would not want to.

And that was always the way he remembered her now.

The old man, Merced, had gone out to his place at the gate. Now when the door to the clubhouse opened, it was two of Hunter's players, two of the young ones, who came in. As a minor league manager, Andrew Hunter caught himself thinking from time to time within the framework of the player roster as it was printed in the four-page program, the program that sold for a dime and contained a lucky number that would be flashed on the scoreboard during the seventh inning. The lucky number was sponsored alternately by some half a dozen Fairchild Street merchants, and entitled the fortunate holder to anything from free gas, oil, and grease at Peconi's Service Station to a ten-dollar merchandise certificate at the Ludlow-Berg department store.

Always, the roster, with the starting players listed in batting order, hung on a wall in Hunter's mind, just like (he once told himself) an eye chart in a doctor's office. It looked like this:

> 5 Whittier, 2b
> 2 Gladstone, 3b
> 1 Hunter (mgr), cf
> 8 Crimeau   9 Gold, c

```
10 Maracz'ki, rf
6 Aloya, 1b
3 Rosch, lf
4 Johnson    14 O'Brien, ss
7 Vincent    11 Williams
        16 Walsh
12 North    15 Masick, p
```

And when a player came into the room or walked through a hotel lobby or boarded the bus, the quiet process of recognition on the part of Andrew Hunter would be not that this was Joe Whittier, but, instead, 5 Whittier, 2b; not that it was Bill O'Brien, but 14 O'Brien, ss. He was aware of this mental custom he had; it amused him, in fact, that he would think of 14 O'Brien, ss, when in truth O'Brien was his utility man and had played practically everywhere except shortstop. It was the custom of the printer who made up the programs to put the utility man on the same line with the eighth man in the batting order, so that automatically whatever was the position that the eighth man played, that also would be the position listed for the utility man. This was done not so much to save space as to accommodate the fans, some of whom had indicated some years before that they did not know the meaning of "ut" after a player's name. It was not too important a point. There seldom was more than one utility man on the squad anyway, and toward the end of the season, when clubs higher in the chain started moving for the pennant and the roster limits were off, Conway would be lucky if it finished out the season without having to recruit players off factory teams or the campus of Conway State Teachers College, which had a baseball team of sorts.

The program that sold for a dime had other special fascinations for Andrew Hunter. He did not know why this was so. It bemused him, for example, to observe that Chet Maraczewski's name was apostrophized to Marac'ki even though there was ample room for spelling it out. He did not quite know why Bo Walsh should have his name centered among the five pitchers, or why, once the printer had set out obviously to list the pitchers in the order of the numbers on their uniforms, he should put 16 Walsh behind 7 Vincent and 11 Williams, but ahead of 12 North and 15 Masick.

Nor did it escape the manager that there was no number 13 on the Bears. That was understandable, inasmuch as the uniforms originated with the parent Philadelphia Bears, whose front office gleaned a small amount of publicity each year by pointing out that 13 was an unlucky number. The Philadelphia press agent had even won a degree of attention the day Bobby Thomson won the '51 pennant for the Giants with his ninth-inning home run against the Dodgers. The story from Philadelphia quoted the Bears' manager as saying that this could never have happened to his club, because it had no number 13—the number of Ralph Branca, who threw the pitch to Thomson.

It was proper, however, for the program to list all five of the Conway pitchers as starters, because they were. When you played four-game series—and, with postponements, they could quickly stretch to five and six games—and you only had five pitchers, you started them all. There were six teams in the Empire League, each of which played a 120-game schedule, meeting each other team twelve times at home and twelve times on the road. That meant the league as a whole would play a total of 360 games in the season, exclusive of playoff games. The schedule was drawn up by Dr. T. T. Yates, a dentist in Conway who was a nut on baseball and statistics. He had explained to Andrew Hunter, before the season began, that you could find out how many games would have to be played in any given league in order for each team to meet each other team once. "You multiply the number of teams by one-less-that-number," he said, "and divide by two." He reached for a piece of paper—he was working on Hunter's teeth at the time—and wrote:

$$S = \frac{n\,(n-1)}{2}$$

"Now," he continued cheerily, "you take the Empire League. Six teams, so n is 6. Six times n-minus-one, which is 5, is 30, and you divide by two and get 15. So there have to be fifteen games for each team to meet each other team once. But each team plays each other team 24 times, twelve at home and twelve away, so you multiply 15 by 24 and you come out with 360." He beamed. "Here, you can take this with you." And he gave Hunter the piece of paper that possessed the magic formula.

Later that night, Andrew Hunter had asked Ed Rosch, his eighteen-year-old left fielder, if he could guess how many games the Empire League as a whole played.

Rosch pondered it briefly. Then he said, "Three hundred and sixty."

"How'd you guess?"

Rosch shrugged. "Each team plays 120 games. Six teams in the league. Six times 120 is 720. Divide by two—360. Simple."

Hunter looked at him. "Why'd you divide by two?"

His fellow outfielder regarded him pityingly. "Because each game is played by two teams."

Next time he had his teeth done, Hunter told himself, he would instruct Dr. Yates as to what he could do with his formula.

All this formed the train of thought that ambled through Stat Hunter's mind—an intelligent but a cluttered mind—as he sat on the bench before his locker, soap on his face, and in his hand the letter from his daughter. All this, just because two of his ballplayers had walked in the door.

They were Luis Aloya, the first baseman, and Simon North, one of the pitchers.

"Hey, there, Stat," Aloya said. "Jee-sus, it's hot in here. What's a-matter with that goddam fan?"

"Watch the language," Hunter said. "Simon, how's the foot?"

"All right," North said. He was the only local boy on the Conway team. "I can pitch tonight."

"Vagrancy's going to pitch," Hunter said. "I want to use you day after tomorrow when Batavia comes in."

"Well, I didn't work since Sunday," North said.

"And you cut the foot Monday," Hunter said. "You can do some running out there tonight before the game. Practice starting and stopping. Go through your motion and then pretend there's a bunted ball to either side and see how you break down off the rubber going for it."

North nodded and went to his locker, across from Hunter's. The lockers were numbered in the order of the uniforms the players wore. Andrew Hunter was at the end of the row nearest the door, and Monk Gladstone was next to him.

Hunter stood up now and opened his locker. He put the letter in the inside pocket of his suit coat and then, leaving the locker door open, went back inside to finish shaving. There was activity around him. The visiting Rome Senators had arrived in the dressing-room to his right. A couple of them came in to use the bathroom and said, "Hey, Stat," and "Goes-a-boy, Stat?" Hunter nodded at them in the mirror and went on shaving, and in his mind now he began to plot tonight's game in advance. It was a necessary thing to do, and besides, it was a way to avoid thinking about the letter from his daughter, Janet, and about his wife, Marian, who had left him two years ago. *No,* his mind amended, *not quite two years. It was in August …*

There would be no need to go over the Rome hitters with his players. They had done this two nights before, Tuesday night, before the four-game series with the Senators began. Now it was Thursday night, and Conway had taken two straight from Rome. The Bears were in second place, four games back of Auburn, which had a club that hit well but which already had dropped two series to the Bears. Stat Hunter liked that. If your club beat the frontrunner with any kind of consistency, then your club had to be sound. He liked that, Hunter did, and he liked the fact that the Bears only once so far this season had lost as many as four games in a row. They were good signs—good signs in the majors, good signs in Class C.

He finished shaving and went back into the locker room; Almost all the players were there now. Two of them—Aloya and North—already had finished dressing and had gone out on the field. Hunter looked around the room and then went to his locker and started putting on his uniform. He looked around again and said, "Where's Vagrancy?"

"Sitting on an ice wagon somewhere," Monk Gladstone said. "He'll show up along about ten minutes before game time."

"He'll show up in time to warm up or I'll know the reason why," Hunter said, half to himself. It occurred to him that this was too righteous a thing to say about a forty-six-year-old pitcher who had been in organized ball when Andrew Hunter was still wearing knickers on the sidewalks of Long Island City. Williams was from the south, somewhere. His hair line was receding, and he had an old man's face with a great crook of a nose, but his arm seemed endlessly supple; and though he waddled when he moved, he still knew the shortest way around the bases.

"Mr. Hunter?"

Stat Hunter looked up. A good thing about the long, the involved, the sometimes dreamy trains of thought that he seemed these days so often to embark upon was that he could snap out of them, return to reality, with speed and without visible effort. Sitting in front of his locker now, lacing on his baseball shoes, he looked up and saw a lean, large-boned man, sharp-faced and with hair that was brown and short-tufted, looking down at him. The man's age was indeterminate. It could have been thirty, or thirty-five, or even forty. He wore a chocolate-brown summer suit and carried a small canvas bag, of the kind that airlines give away to their overseas passengers.

He said now, "I'm Walt Corio. Mr. Kelly said I ought to see you about suiting up."

From time to time, Kelly, the club's general manager, would sign on new players on a trial basis. Though they carried only fifteen men regularly, the Bears, as a Class C team, were entitled to carry seventeen.

There was something about the new man that Andrew Hunter, instinctively, did not like: something about the way the eyes looked.

"Kelly sign you?" Hunter asked now. "I haven't seen him in the past couple of days."

"He's paying my expenses for a week," the man named Corio said. "I told him that'd be all right. I'm trying to get back into ball."

"Get back in?"

"I been in factory work. Played some first base for a while in Tennessee and Kentucky."

"Organized ball?"

Corio nodded.

"Play anywhere else?"

Corio understood the question. "Sure. I'm right-handed when I throw. Bat left."

"Hit a ball?"

"All I want is a try."

Hunter finished with his shoes and stood up. "All right. Go out and see the old man on the gate. His name's Merced. Get the keys from him, and you can have one of the extra suits. I want to see you hit when you get dressed."

The manager stood up, took his black leather glove from the shelf of his locker, and went out the door that led along a dirt runway underneath the stands to the Bears' dugout. When he got there, eight or ten of the Bears already were on the field, taking batting practice. Arnold Margolies, the sports editor of the Conway *Times,* was sitting on the bench in the dugout, one leg flexed up beside him, idly socking his right hand into the glove he had put on. He said, "Hey, Stat, Waterloo's winning the first."

"Big?" Hunter said.

"Four to one in the fifth," Margolies said. The Waterloo team was playing league-leading Auburn tonight in a twilight-night double header.

"Well, all right," Hunter said. "How's Sylvia tonight?"

"Same as ever." Margolies was a plump, preoccupied young man. "She's three days overdue."

"My wife was a week overdue before she had our little girl."

Margolies stopped punching the glove. "I didn't know you were married, Stat."

"I'm not," Hunter said, "now."

"No?"

"No," Hunter said. "What are you looking at me that way for?"

"I'm not looking at you any way." Margolies went back to punching the glove. After a moment, he shrugged his shoulders. "I'm a newspaperman."

"Well, you want to do me a favor, leave it alone," Hunter said.

"Sure," Margolies said. "You want a stick of gum, Stat?"

"No," the manager said.

"It's Beeman's Pepsin," Margolies said.

"No, thanks," Hunter said, and he went on the field and walked over to the batting cage. Oscar Johnson, his shortstop, was taking hitting practice. A couple of the kids from the factory team at Whitemarsh, the town up the highway from Conway, were doing the pitching and catching. They wore their own uniforms, gray with blue lettering. It irritated Hunter. The least he would have liked, after all those years in the big league, would have been to have the team he managed look like a professional outfit. He himself always wore the red-and-white striped socks and, except on very hot nights such as tonight, the red, long-sleeved undershirt, to match the red-script *Bears* that ran across the shirtfronts of the Conway team's white home uniforms. But some of the players wore nothing but ankle-length white sweat socks, and some of them had blue or gray or black undershirts; and the team's equipment trunk was hardly luxurious enough for Hunter to complain.

Leaning against the back of the batting cage now, Hunter said, "Let's see you hit the inside pitch to right field, Oscar." He cupped his right hand around his mouth and called to the kid who was pitching, "Pitch him inside."

The kid came in too close with the next two pitches. Then he got one reasonably where it was supposed to be, and Johnson, the shortstop, laced it into right field.

"How was that, Stat?"

"No good," Hunter said. "You shifted your front foot, long before the pitch came. It'd be obvious to anybody what you had in mind."

"That's because I knew it was going to be inside," the shortstop said.

"That's some reasoning," Hunter said.

A scattering of sound came now from the stands. The visiting Rome Senators were coming on the field, and the several hundred fans were greeting them with that peculiar brand of minor-league intimacy that makes every fan a bench jockey. One of the Rome players came over to the cage with a bat in his hands, and Hunter turned and looked at him. "We got twenty minutes yet."

"I know it, Stat," the other player said. "I'm gonna have my picture took, is all, and I thought I'd come over here."

"Well, take it over there," Hunter said.

Chet Maraczewski, Conway's right fielder, came and stood beside Hunter back of the batting cage, his foot up on the base of the frame, his left hand intertwined with the webbing, in perfect reproduction of the manager's pose. Together they watched Joe Whittier taking his clean, incisive cuts at bat. Finally Maraczewski said, "I was talking to Luis. I'd like to try that play."

"The one I used last night?"

Maraczewski nodded and spat professionally into the dirt. He was nineteen years old, and last night he had seen Stat Hunter field a single and throw the ball on a line to Aloya at first base, catching the Rome runner after he had made his turn.

"It takes practice," Hunter said now. "The only time you can make it is when the runner comes to a complete stop, and then he's got to have turned far enough to give you a play."

"Why does he have to come to a stop? I mean, why do I have to wait for him?"

"Because if he doesn't and he sees a throw back to first, he'll just keep going. Stan Hack did it to Mel Ott the year the Cubs won the pennant last, and Ott had it down to a science. But when he threw the ball, Hack just kept going and Weintraub missed the bounce at first and Hack wound up on third."

"Well, I'd talk it over with my first baseman first," Maraczewski said.

"You talk it over with your catcher, too," Hunter said. "And don't pull it with a man on base."

Chet Maraczewski licked his lips. "It'd be a hell of a play with a man on first—assuming you couldn't get him going into third, or say there's two outs at the time. The hitter would never expect it."

"No," Hunter said, "he wouldn't. But who backs up your throw? The catcher. So if the throw's bad, the catcher gets it, and who's covering home plate?"

Maraczewski spat again. "Nobody."

"All right," Hunter said. "But I'm glad you're thinking of it, and I want you to practice it. It is a good play." He smiled at the young outfielder. "And remember one other thing."

"What's that, Stat?"

"It's this. You're not the only outfielder who's thinking about that play. Some day you'll be a runner on first, or the guy who hits the ball, and they may try it on you. Don't round first base wondering whether the outfielder's going to get your hit. Assume he's going to field it the right way. If he doesn't, you can always go for that extra base. If he does, you won't get caught."

"Why can't I do what Hack did, like you were saying? Con him into throwing back to first and then take off for second?

"You can," Hunter said, "but only after you know the men you're playing against. Hack took a chance not on Ott's fielding ability in right field but on Weintraub's at first base. But even if Weintraub makes a perfect play, it's still going to be close at second base, and Hack figured he had the percentages going with him."

"This is the damnedest business I ever heard of," Maraczewski said.

"Who's hitting next? You?"

"The new guy," Maraczewski said. "Walt Corio."

"That's right," Hunter said. "I want to see him." Inwardly, he admired young Maraczewski for being able to remember the new man's name. It was something he himself was seldom able to do.

Corio knew how to hit—against this pitching, anyway. He swatted a couple on a line, and then he hit the ball over the fence and onto the railroad tracks, a shot of three hundred and fifty feet or more, and in the stands some of the fans started to shout. "Hey, Babe!" one of them yelled.

Monk Gladstone came up to Hunter. He was chewing tobacco, and the effort distended his cheek. "Stat, I've run into this guy someplace before."

Hunter nodded. It was very possible that Gladstone had run into Corio someplace else. On the other hand, it seemed part and parcel of being an old ballplayer that you remembered things whether they were true or not. George Crimeau, the catcher, had memories of big-league games he never played in; Monk Gladstone, the third baseman, remembered people he had never met; Vagrancy Williams, the pitcher, remembered women he had never had. Hunter wondered when it would start happening to him. As of the moment, his memory was sharp—too sharp, as evidenced in the way he had spoken to Margolies, the sports editor, remembering the way Janet had been born. Again now, he had to force it from his mind, and he said aloud to Gladstone, "You play against him?"

"I don't know," Gladstone said, watching Corio hit. "He's familiar, that's all. I didn't remember him when he came in the clubhouse, but watching him hit a ball, it's different. You know?"

"Yes," the manager said. He looked to his right and saw Lester Kelly, the team's general manager, sitting in the dugout. Stat Hunter went over to him and said, "This one hits a hell of a ball."

"I know," Kelly said. He sat, tall and completely relaxed, on the bench. "He's on trial for a week. He's with the team. You can use him tonight."

"You took care of that?"

Kelly nodded. "He said he'd had some experience."

"Know anything more about him?"

"Hell, no," Kelly said. "We had room for him, so I told him all right for a week."

"Well, we can use a left-handed hitter," Hunter said. He turned to watch the new man, Corio, put one off the fence in right field. "He sure does pull a ball."

"He said he played first base," Kelly said.

"He throws right," the manager said. "I could use him anywhere. I might use him on first. Aloya doesn't hit them too long."

"So long as you don't use him at second base," Kelly said. He did not have to say any more. Joe Whittier was the white hope. Joe Whittier had just turned twenty. He was agile, fast, and smart. He had a cartilage condition in his right knee which made him draft-exempt. The Philadelphia Bears knew all about him. Marcus, the scout, was not visiting Conway for his health. Hadn't the Chicago Cubs brought up Roy Smalley from Class C to the majors without any stops, and hadn't Smalley paid off? Whittier was hitting .344, as of now, and he led the league in runs batted in, a startling accomplishment for a lead-off man. Stat Hunter was using him first in the batting order not only because of his speed and his skill at getting on base, but because a lead-off man was in a position where he would learn faster, and because in the long run he would come to bat more frequently. That was why the truly great sluggers, like Ruth and Williams, batted third in the lineup. True, they had good hitters coming up behind them. But by batting third, instead of cleanup, they increased by just that much the chance that they would come to bat again in the ninth inning. And it was something for the other team to think about before giving them an intentional base on balls.

None of this really moved consciously through Andrew Hunter's mind—not unless, as in the case of Chet Maraczewski, his right fielder, he wanted to explain a certain play in detail. It was enough that you knew what there was to know. You watched for a signal before the first pitch to a batter, knowing that most clubs put their signals on one pitch in advance, and then you watched for the signal before the second pitch, and if there was a signal, and if the batter did not do what you expected him to do, then you reasoned that the second signal had canceled the first. It did not do you any good, but you stored it in your memory, and weeks later, when you had your first baseman moving in to field the bunt when the bunt would not ordinarily be expected, you had the payoff. But it was not something you thought of consciously. You did it because it was part of what you did, if you were a good baseball man.

And yet, when you talked to someone like young Maraczewski, and explained why a thing was done or was not done, sometimes you surprised even yourself. The world was full of surprises. *Dear Daddy ... Mommy said I could have a surprise. Not a kitten or a dog but a real live ... GUESS??*

"Say, Les," Hunter said, looking down at the general manager in the dugout. "If an eight-year-old girl told you she was going to get a surprise and it wasn't a cat or a dog, what would it be?"

With almost anyone but Kelly, a question such as this would have invited some sort of gratuitously obscene response, but Lester Kelly was not like that.

"Why," he said, "offhand, I'd say a pony."

"A pony?"

"That's what I said. How'd we get on the subject of ponies? What were we talking about? Joe Whittier."

"I don't think he's too fond of me," Hunter said.

"Neither do I. He's a fresh punk and he thinks he knows everything there is to know about baseball."

The manager nodded. "There's something else, too."

Kelly looked at him, wondering whether Hunter had found out about Whittier's gambling debts—not that he, Kelly, did not want Hunter to know, but because he thought that so long as his play on the field continued excellent, Whittier should be given a chance to get himself off the hook.

But Hunter was not talking about the gambling. "He's got a girl, Les. A girl named Jo Ann. Far as I can tell, she likes anything in a baseball suit. She's stopped me and tossed herself around a little two or three times. Now she's going around with Joe. I think maybe he's got some idea I'm competition."

"Well, if you haven't even had a real date with her, what would make him think that?"

Hunter shrugged. "Maybe something she told him."

CHAPTER TWO
NOTHING AND ONE

Auburn, leading the Empire League, had lost the first
game to Waterloo and was losing the second. It was a chance
for Conway to pick up a game and a half, and, out in center field,
Andrew Hunter swore to himself that from now on Vagrancy
Williams was going to show up half an hour ahead of game
time on nights when he was scheduled to pitch. Williams had
arrived with time remaining for no more than six or eight warm-
up throws. Twice during the first inning, Stat Hunter had come
in to argue with the umpires, so Williams could have time to
throw some more, but Vagrancy still was off. He had walked six
men, and Conway trailed Rome 5 to 1 now, in the top of the fifth
inning.

A small, self-elected cheering section among the fans back
of third base had set up a kind of reciprocal salute for Vagrancy
Williams. As he wound up to pitch, half of the chorus would
cry out, "Hey, Will-yums!" Then, whenever the umpire called
it a ball, the other half would shout at Vagrancy, "You stink!"
Vagrancy did not appreciate the recognition. It did not particu-
larly help his pitching, either. He went to three and nothing on
the first man up, and in center field, Stat Hunter looked over at
his bullpen, where Art Vincent and Harry Masick were sitting,
along with Phil Gold the catcher, and wagged with his glove. The

second time he did it, he caught their attention, and Vincent got up and started throwing to Gold.

The Rome batsman got his walk, and on the next pitch Williams threw, he lit out for second base. Automatically, Andrew Hunter moved in to back up the peg from George Crimeau. Joe Whittier moved over to take it, but he was in back of the bag, and the runner slid to the left side and hooked in ahead of the tag. The play was close enough for Whittier to say something to Cross-Eyed Collins, the base umpire. Collins looked out to center field and said, "Shut this one up, Stat. The man was safe."

"How do you know?" Hunter responded, but he did not move to join the disagreement, and Whittier knew better than to take it on himself. He still was not good at coming into position to take a throw and make a tag. Too often he played it safe, back of the base, and it was hard to convince him he should change, because there were not many good baserunners in the Empire League, and he was a match for most of them even when he played it wrong.

The man who was at bat now put the next pitch on one bounce into center field for a single. Stat Hunter took it coming in. His right foot struck the ground as his glove fielded the ball, and in the next stride he was throwing for the plate. Even in the reflex speed of the play, he was the manager, the onlooker, and it gratified him to see that Luis Aloya, the first baseman, had not moved into the cutoff slot.

The throw went on one bounce to George Crimeau. Ol' George tagged the runner with a barehand sweep and wound up, still crouched, arm cocked threateningly toward the man who had hit the ball. The hitter stayed at first base.

On the mound, Vagrancy Williams talked mournfully to himself and went to work on the next batter. He walked him, and, in center field, Stat Hunter called for time and waved for Art Vincent to come in and pitch.

The manager joined Williams and Crimeau at the mound, waiting for Vincent to get there. "You got to warm up more than you did tonight," he said to Williams. "You get us in a jam with those bases on balls."

"That umpire back of the plate ain't nothing to phone home about," Vagrancy said.

"He's right, Stat," ol' George said. "The umpirin' heah ain' what we used to have in th' *big* league."

"The umpire's not that far off," Hunter said. "I can see the pitches."

"Cain't see nothing with these lights," Vagrancy Williams said.

Art Vincent joined them, and Hunter gave him the ball. He said, "Let's not walk any of these men, Art."

Vincent was a tall, terribly emaciated-looking young man who taught music at a small-town high school in western New York. All summer long, he played baseball for the Bears. He did not aspire to higher prominence in the hierarchy of the game, or even higher pay. Pitching for Conway suited him. Occasionally, it suited Conway, too.

George Crimeau went back to catch Vincent's warmup throws, and Andrew Hunter stood on the mound, watching his new pitcher work. Vagrancy Williams, talking to himself once more, shuffled to the dugout, and the fans gave him one farewell chorus:

"Hey, Will-yums!"

"You stink!"

Vincent got the Bears out of the inning, and Hunter was glad he had made the pitching change when he did, even though Vincent would be first at bat for the Bears in the last of the fifth.

Vincent did not hit well, and this time he did not even offer at the ball, striking out on four pitches.

Then Joe Whittier got up. He dropped the first pitch down the third-base line. It was a bunt that had English on it and it might have rolled foul, but the Rome third baseman did not give it that chance. He grabbed it barehanded and threw to first—threw high and wide, and Whittier went into second base standing up.

That's the trouble in this league, Stat Hunter told himself. *They make it all right for you so you think you have nothing left to learn.* The froggy public address system growled, "Error. Error." Hunter looked to second base and saw Whittier paw the dirt momentarily in irritation. Joe Whittier counted his base hits. He had his eye on the big league, and Hunter could not blame him. Still, the manager was inwardly amused, as much by the public-address announcer as by anything. The combination of the announcer, a frustrated radio crooner who by day worked as a technician at WCWY, the Conway station, and the public address system itself could bring forth some interesting results. The announcer had particular trouble with the letter *p*. Always, it came out over the loudspeaker as *puh*. Monk Gladstone told Hunter that a year ago some local comedian had asked the announcer to page Peter Papapopolus. "It wrecked the p.a. works for a month," Gladstone said.

Gladstone was at bat now. He got a walk, and now it was the Rome bullpen that began heating up. Stat Hunter stepped in. He singled to right on the third pitch, and Simon North, the Bears' pitcher who was idle tonight and thus was stationed in the coaching box back of third, held Whittier up. Stat Hunter told himself he would have had Whittier go for home, but he did not blame young North for playing it safe. Whittier could have made it home, and on the throw-in, Gladstone could have gone to third and maybe even Hunter himself to second, but Conway was behind by four runs, and if Whittier had been out at home, Simon North knew there would be hell to pay.

Bases were loaded, therefore, and George Crimeau was up. He flied fairly deep to left field, and Whittier scored after the catch. Two were out now, and when Chet Maraczewski walked, loading the bases again, the Rome team still did not make a move to change its pitcher. Luis Aloya, the first baseman, was coming up for Conway, and he had struck out twice tonight.

Stat Hunter called time, and moved off second base, gesturing toward the dugout. Aloya got the idea and turned back, and Corio, the new man, came out to hit. There was a consultation with the plate umpire and the field announcer, and then the p.a. system crackled to life and said, "Number Eighteen, Walt Corio, not on your puh-rogram, buh-atting for Aloya. Corio."

The manager of the Rome team, who played first base, came over to talk to his pitcher and catcher. They did not look at Corio as they talked. Then they took their positions, and the pitcher, throwing without windup, came in high and inside.

Corio hit it with a certain even grace, so that it did not seem much of an effort. The ball carried on a vast, soaring arc, striking off the top of the fence in right-center field and bounding back and away from the center fielder. Three runs came in and Corio stopped at third, standing up. The fans were shouting in excitement.

Now Rome did change pitchers. The new man was a young, scared-looking lefthander with an immense, awkward motion. He had a fast ball that was quite fast. On the first pitch to Ed Rosch, the Bears' left fielder, the southpaw kicked high, came down, and realized only then, in the very motion of releasing the ball, that the man on third was stealing home on him. His throw to the plate was creditable but late, and Corio was home in the dust, putting Conway in front, 6 to 5.

Then in the next inning, the sixth, Joe Whittier hit a home run with a man on, making it 8 to 5. Rome got a run in the ninth, but Hunter kept Vincent in there, and the relief man got the side out. Conway had the game. Auburn had lost two, and now Auburn's lead was down to two and a half games.

The scoreboard in left field was new and electric, running between two soot-blackened light poles. It told the story:

VIS.	2 1 0 2 0 0 0 0 1	6 8 3
CNWY.	1 0 0 0 5 2 0 0	8 9 1

Looking at it as he left the field, Stat Hunter realized that Vincent, the music-teaching relief pitcher who did not give a damn, would be credited with the victory, while Vagrancy Williams, who had pitched four and one-third innings, would go around muttering to himself about the injustices wrought by tyro sports writers who scored the games. Hunter grinned. It had been a good game to win. It was a game they could all take credit for—even Simon North, coaching at third, for having held Whittier up in that big inning. The number of times that would have paid off for a five-run inning ... well, his own life, Stat Hunter told himself at times, was little more than a series of numbers. If not numbers on the scoreboard, then numbers someplace else—the box score, perhaps, which tomorrow morning would say:

Hunter, cf.   4   2   2   5   1

That's you, he told himself, *Hunter, cf.* Then he went down into the dugout and along the runway to the dressing-room, with the

THE ONLY GAME IN TOWN

noise of the players and the whine of the electric fan and the hissing sound of the showers.

He found the new man, Corio, talking to George Crimeau.

"Man," ol' George said as Hunter came up to them, "this boy can hit a *ball!*"

"That was a long one," Hunter said.

"Man," Crimeau said, "I don't know when I *seen* a ball hit like ol' Wally heah hit that ball, and I seen plenty of long balls in th' *big* league."

"Wally?" Hunter said. "Is it Wally?"

"Walt," the new man, Corio, said. His voice was soft and Southern.

"Well," Hunter said, "just to get it understood once and for all, we steal home on a sign on this club, not when we feel like it."

"What? You sore because I stole home?"

"Not sore. We just don't want to see it again. We're trying to teach baseball to the young players on this club, and signals are part of baseball."

"But that was the lead run."

"I don't care what run it was."

" 'Course," George Crimeau said, "not that I want to take anythin' away from *Wally* heah, but I hope you observed how ol' George put th' *ball* on that runner after that hit out to ol' Stat."

"That was a beaut, George," Hunter said.

Corio set his lips and went down the line to his locker. Monk Gladstone said, "See where they stole another base on you, George," but he was not being nasty about it.

"That boy at second base goin' have to learn how to make that *tag*," Crimeau said. "Ain't no good just standin' there 'th the *ball*, arguin' with th' *um*pire. Hey, there, young Joe." He waved a sweaty fist at Joe Whittier. "You goin' have to watch ol' *George*, find out how you make a tag."

Whittier grinned at him. His home run had been his ninth of the year, and his first in more than a week.

"Well," Crimeau said, "ol' George got th' heats for *good* tonight. Man, I don't know when I *seen* it so hot, and *I* seen it when it was *hot*."

"In the *big* league," Monk Gladstone said.

"Big or little, don't make no difference with ol' George," Crimeau said.

Andrew Hunter, the manager, always was a part of this informal court after a game. For one thing, he had not yet become able to accustom himself to using the same shower with players from the opposing team.

As a result, he invariably sat on the bench before his locker until the shower room was clear. That made him the last to leave.

He was sitting there now when Joe Whittier came back from the shower room. Hunter said, "Joe, got a minute? I want to talk to you."

"What about?"

"About making the tag at second base."

"Don't like the way I do it? You sound like ol' George."

"Never mind who I sound like. You want to hear about how to make the tag right or not?"

"Not tonight," Whittier said. "Haven't got time."

"Got a date?"

Whittier looked at him. "I had one, but my car broke down, so I'm getting a lift home and I gotta hurry. You know? Otherwise the guy won't wait."

"I can drive you home."

"No, thanks," Whittier said, and moved away.

The only man in the lavatory when Hunter finally went in there was Harry Masick, the pitcher, who had warmed up in the bullpen when Art Vincent ran into that little trouble in the ninth. Masick was a small, extremely hairy man. Hunter said to him, "You're going tomorrow night, Harry. Then when Batavia comes in Saturday it'll be Simon and Bo Walsh."

Masick nodded. "I didn't feel so sharp out there tonight, Stat."

"Well, we might have needed you in the ninth," the manager said, "but it worked out the other way."

"Just as well," Masick said. He made a face. "My wife's waiting for me down at the motel. She's mad as hell at me about something."

"Well, tell her you're only two and a half games out."

"That what you used to tell your wife, Stat?"

Hunter looked at him. "What does that mean?"

"Nothing," Masick said.

"Well," the manager said, "it doesn't make one way or the other, actually." He went and stood under the shower.

Occasionally Andrew Hunter sang under the shower. It did not have any particular bearing on whether he was happy or not happy at the time; sometimes he sang and sometimes he did not sing. But he liked it better when he was alone. In the apartment they had had in Chicago, he and Marian had the various albums of records from the Broadway shows. One of them Andrew Hunter liked especially. It was a song from *Carousel,* and now he sang the words, and was faithful to the tune, as far as he remembered:

> "My little girl,
> Pink and white
> As peaches and cream is she...."

He was still singing, dressing in front of his locker, alone in the room, when old Jack Merced, the caretaker, came in to close up.

"Hey, Stat," the old man said. "That was some ball game."

"They're always good when you win them," Hunter said.

"That new man really hit that ball," Merced said. He went over and shut off the fan. Two houseflies were chasing each other noisily in the light from the shower room. "Where'd you pick him up, Stat?"

"Kelly found him. I don't know much about him."

"Any of the boys know him?"

"No," Hunter said. "Monk Gladstone said he'd seen him someplace, but he didn't remember where."

"Stranger, hey?" the old man said. "Well, he's going to be all right. You just watch him go."

"He hit us a big one tonight," Hunter said.

"We drew damn close to a thousand tonight, too," the old man said. "It was a good night all around. Did you get that letter, Stat?"

"You gave it to me," Hunter said.

"Well," Merced said, "tomorrow or the next day Marcus gets to town."

"He won't see much this trip."

"Why? What about young Joe?"

"Give young Joe two more months," Hunter said. "Let him learn something about running bases. Half a dozen other things."

"Well, all right," the old man said. "Maybe this new man can teach him a thing or two. I noted they drove off together in young Joe's car."

"Whittier's car?"

"That's what I said. You want to turn out the light, Stat, and turn that thing on the lock from the inside when you go?"

Hunter nodded absently.

"Good night," the old man said, and he went out.

Hunter finished dressing, thinking about old Jack Merced and about Marcus, the Philadelphia scout who was coming to town, and about Joe Whittier, and the new man, Corio, and what the story was that Whittier had given him about the car. He was thinking that Monk Gladstone had seen Corio someplace before, and thinking that that throw to first base last night and the one to the plate tonight had left the Hunter arm tight, needing warmth, needing time to snap back—needing so much time that tomorrow night, he knew, he would hardly be able to throw at all. And thinking of arms and warmth and time made him remember his daughter and Marian, his wife—he would never think of her as his ex-wife—and then he thought of Joe Whittier's girl, Jo Ann, and he turned off the light in the clubhouse and went out, remembering to fix the lock from the inside the way Merced, the old man, had told him to do.

It was just a little before midnight when Walt Corio and Joe Whittier drove up to the Black Widow, a formidably entitled place on the highway that ran from Conway to the west. They drove up in Whittier's car, the one Whittier had told Hunter was on the fritz. The friendship between Whittier and Corio had been instant, bred of what Corio had heard Whittier tell Lester Kelly in Kelly's office that afternoon, bred of what the bartender had told Corio about young Joe. Whittier was young enough to regard the older man's interest as a form of esteem. They made a congenial twosome.

"A bartender told me to ask for downstairs," Corio said. They had left the car in the parking lot out back. The Black Widow had neon-ribbed windows all around. It was built to the square, garish pattern of the roadhouse, with a portico in front, a portico that in the winter was enclosed by storm doors to provide a comfortable entrance for year-round custom.

"Never mind asking for anything," Whittier said to Corio. "Come on with me, is all. How much you got?"

"Enough."

"How much?"

Walt Corio's voice did not change. It was still Southern and smooth, and terribly polite in its sound and nuance. "Enough."

They went inside and Whittier said, "Enough to lend me some?"

"How much you got?"

"A lousy twenty."

"See how you do."

Whittier did not say anything. From the foyer inside he moved expertly past the hatcheck booth, into what seemed to Corio a black and foreboding areaway. Corio followed and saw a blue light ahead. The light was over a narrow stairway that led down. At the foot of the stairs there was a door that opened away from them and, following the young second baseman, Corio found himself in a low-ceilinged, grimly bare room. There were three tables, at two of which sat men and women, playing cards. The third table, over by the far wall, was the dice table. Here nobody sat—all were standing, even the house man, a small, gray man in shirtsleeves who stood between the table and the wall, watching the play carefully, with a patient smile on his face. Joe Whittier and Walt Corio came to this table; a very large table it was, with perhaps twenty people grouped around it, most of them men, but women too—four or five women, dressed in the sheer clothes of summer. The air was surprisingly clear: two giant full-stand electric fans rotated at opposite ends of the room. They, and the tables, were the only furnishings.

The dice game was one typical for that part of the state. The dice moved clockwise around the table, and when you shot, you played the house, at the established odds. If you wanted to bet against the shooter, you told him what the bet was and he took you on the side or refused; or you could bet with the shooter against the house; or non-shooters might bet among themselves as to how the dice would fall. Of this last, the house took no cognizance. The house man was concerned with the man or woman who had the dice. The odds were established. The house had to win—sooner or later.

Corio studied the faces at the table. He did not worry that he would be recognized, but he wondered how Whittier got away with it. The answer—the only answer—was that the people who shot dice and played cards in the basement at the Black Widow were not the people who went out to see the Conway Bears play in the Empire League, and it figured.

Still, there was a risk; but it seemed not to bother Joe Whittier. When it came his turn he put a five-dollar bill on the table and threw the dice against the opposite rim. They came up nine, and the table became quietly alive with muttered observations. "Says he doesn't nine." "He sixes first." "Says he does." Money showed.

A large man in shirtsleeves and blue suspenders worked his way around the outside of the circle of dice players, talking briefly to each one. When he got to Walt Corio, he said, "You, sir?"

"Me, sir?" Corio said. "Who are you?"

"Waiter, sir," the man said. "Something?"

"Beer," Corio said. "You got Miller's?"

"Miller's," the waiter repeated, and moved on past Joe Whittier. Corio assumed it was a custom for the waiter to skip the man who held the dice.

In the case of Joe Whittier, concentrated application did no good. He sevened after two more throws, and the dice passed to Corio.

Corio picked them up, looked at them, then handed them to the man on his left.

"Go ahead," he said.

"What's the matter with the dice, mister?"

"Nothing," Corio said.

"You looked at them funny," the man on his left said.

"I never touch the dice," Corio said.

"Then why'd you look at them?"

"Old habit."

The house man on the other side of the table said, "Your pleasure, sir." The smile did not leave his face.

The man on Corio's left muttered something, then took the dice and put a ten-dollar bill down on the table. As smoothly processed as an automatic gear shift, heads leaned forward to watch.

Joe Whittier watched Corio. Corio bet only house odds, and always against the shooter. At times, he did not bet at all. He might bet against a six or an eight but not against a nine or a five; and he did not, as some at the table did, bet against the shooter before the dice were thrown. Even with his comparative youth, Whittier could understand what Corio was doing. He was playing dice the only way dice profitably can be played: setting himself up, in effect, as an auxiliary house man, betting always against the roll and always after it, so that he was additionally protected against a hot run of passes.

What Whittier could not understand was why Corio would do this in such a relatively small game, where he would have to stay at the table over a long stretch of time to make any kind of money. It did not occur to him that this was the only way Walt Corio gambled.

Playing against the house was Corio's mission in life. Now less than half an hour had gone by, and Whittier was down to five dollars. Corio had made a little—a very little—and the dice were on the other side of the table.

Corio's voice was so low that only Whittier could hear. "You running out, Joe?"

Whittier nodded.

"You in deep in this town?"

"Pretty. Why?"

"Thought you might like to get out, is all."

"How?"

Corio smiled at him. He knew how much money would be bet on baseball in a league the size of the Empire League … not enough for one game; but a game here and there, four or five or six in the season, would furnish the cushion Walt Corio wanted. His own baseball career was proscribed: here in Class C he was safe, at least for a while. Meanwhile, there was the need for money.

It would take more than one man, though. Whittier, nonetheless, was an excellent starting point.

Corio was still smiling when a man in a tuxedo came up to Whittier and said, in what would be described as a husky whisper, "Joe. Joe."

Whittier turned.

"Stat Hunter's upstairs," the tuxedo said. "With your broad."

Whittier said nothing for a moment. Then he turned to Walt Corio with a chilled smile. "How do you like that? *One* night—"

"Does he know you're here?" Corio cut in. "What are you going to do? Go upstairs and clap him and have it in the papers in the morning? Come on, buddy, make sense."

"I'm not afraid of him," Whittier said.

"I didn't say you were," Corio said. "Which way is out of here?"

The man in the tuxedo said, "Did you want to use the bulkhead door over at the side? That way you don't have to go up again."

"That's us," Corio said.

❧   ❧   ❧

It took Andrew Hunter a while, when he got home, to adjust to the business at hand. The clock on the bureau in his furnished room said it was one-thirty in the morning, and on the little black table that he used as a desk there was a pile of white paper headed MANAGER's REPORT. Hunter had fallen three days behind on his reports—he was supposed to make one out as soon after each game as the newspaper account of the game became available, so he could clip out the box score and mail it to Philadelphia along with his own comments.

Now, staring at the blank sheet in front of him with its several mimeographed headings, such as DATE and CLUB and OPP. CLUB and SCORE and STANDING, the rest of it blank, up to him to fill in—looking at it, Hunter felt a thrust of futility, and he knew he would do no work tonight.

Some people, Stat Hunter said to himself, ruled governments; others wrote poetry, or guided great airplanes with microphones in control towers, or fixed telegraph wires, or were surgeons or automobile dealers or career soldiers. Some men guided the lives of younger men, as a father might do, and it might have been said of Stat Hunter, a failure as a father, that he was fulfilling a worthy mission as manager of a baseball team. Only tonight he had found out about Joe Whittier, found out so easily that it could only be that Whittier did not care if he knew or not; and he did not know what to do about it.

There had been the girl, Jo Ann, who was Whittier's girl and who had appealed to Hunter in a physical way as he had told himself he could never be attracted again. And that complicated things.

"You're late," she had said, and she was only a voice then. The voice had come quietly from the darkness outside the door when Hunter left the ball park.

"Oh," the manager had said. "Jo Ann. Hi. What are you doing here?"

"Stood up," she said. "So I figured I'd wait for you. Only way to get a date with Mr. Manager."

"And the world do move," Hunter said.

"It sure do," the girl said. "Is it all right with you?"

"Sure," he said. "I'll take you home."

She was wearing a sun dress, with her hair done up in back and without stockings but with high heels. She walked side by side with him to his car, and she had a way that made him feel that even though they were not touching he still was holding her to him.

He said, "I'm surprised at Joe."

"Really?"

Hunter said nothing. He drove a two-door, 1951 Dodge sedan, and he held open the door for her, then went around the front and got in beside her.

"I've been waiting for this," she said.

"Sounds bad."

"It's not bad. From the two or three times we've talked, I wanted to know you a whole lot better. Is that bad?"

"It's tough you got stood up."

The girl looked at him. "I'm just as happy. Is it all right for me to say that?"

"Sure."

"And I don't want to go home."

"No?"

"Not right away. I want a drink. What about you, Mr. Manager. Drink?"

Hunter started the engine. "Sometimes. Where do you want to go?"

"Maybe you've got a place in mind."

"No," he said, "I'm not a fan of any particular one."

"Some things you're not a fan of at all," the girl said. "Are you, Mr. Manager?"

"Some people don't call me Mr. Manager," Hunter said.

"Joe does."

"He does?"

"He sure does," she said. "I know a lot about you. Here, turn left. We can go out to the Black Widow."

"Isn't that a roadhouse?"

"Yes," Jo Ann said, "and I'm Carrie Nation."

"You talk like you knew a lot about the things I don't know about," Hunter said. He put the car on the highway. "No offense."

"Quit it," the girl said. "Let's have fun. I can forget Joe and you can forget your wife and we can have fun."

"Everybody knows everything about my wife tonight," Stat Hunter said. "How is she?"

"Stat," the girl said. "I'm going to call you Stat. I like you, Stat. Let's have fun tonight. Do you want to?"

"Sure," Andrew Hunter said. "While the cat's away. While Joe's having his car fixed."

"There's nothing wrong with his car."

"I know it."

She looked at his face in the dim light from the dashboard. "Joe wanted to shoot dice," she said, and Hunter realized that she was not really exposing Joe Whittier; that she was talking now as much to herself as to him.

But he wanted to know more. "He does that a lot?"

"Yes," she said.

"Win much?"

"He owes more than two thousand dollars."

Hunter flicked his road beams twice at an oncoming car, but the other driver would not lower his lights. "All right," he said softly. "I didn't know it and now I know it and all right. Let's have fun like you say."

Jo Ann said, "He's a good baseball player." She said it defensively.

"He could be even better. He could be great." Hunter licked his lips. "Does he drink too?"

"Some," she said.

"Well, all right," he said. "Who does he owe?"

"What do you mean?"

"Who does he owe the money to? Gamblers? Friendly games? The house somewhere? Professionals? Or don't you know?"

"I don't know," she said. "He just owes the money to people. What difference does it make?"

"All the difference," Hunter said. "If he owes money to the wrong man, somebody might start suggesting to him that the way to get even is to play bad baseball."

"I don't understand."

"Dump the games," Stat Hunter said unhappily. "The hell with it. Who'd he go out with tonight? That new man? Corio?"

"I met him today," Jo Ann said. "He's a good-looking fellow."

"No high-schooler," Hunter said.

"No," she said. "I'd say about your age."

"You like the mature type, hey?"

"Sometimes," she said, and she stretched her long, young body so the legs were out straight and hard. "This is it right up here with the lights. You can park right out front."

"I'd like to find out about that Corio," Hunter said, and swung in before the Black Widow. "Damned if I wouldn't."

"So would I," the girl said.

They got a table inside, and Jo Ann ordered a daiquiri. Andrew Hunter had Old Taylor and water. He said, "Well, here's to us."

CHARLES EINSTEIN

"To you and me," she said, watching him as she sipped from the glass.

"Is your boy friend liable to walk in?"

She put her glass down and began to laugh. She was thinking that he was probably there already, downstairs. But Stat didn't need to know that.

"What's so funny?"

"Nothing," she said. "No, he isn't liable to walk in."

"He said he was going home to bed."

"Stat," the girl said, "you know what you are? You're a nice guy. A *nice guy.*"

"That's what everybody says." Hunter looked at his whisky. "You don't know how tired you get every once in a while, being a nice guy."

"Does everybody say you're a nice guy?"

"Everybody," Andrew Hunter said.

They fell silent for a time. "I'm really not much company," Hunter said at last. "A girl like you could have done a lot better."

"You think so?" she asked, and then: "Do you want to talk about her?"

"Who? Marian?"

"Is that her name? Marian?"

Her saying that, the way she said it, made Hunter want to talk. If he had stopped to reason it through, he would have known why. It had been Jo Ann's simple use of the present tense, when she said, *Is that her name?* Most people, talking about your ex-wife, would say *was.* The way she said it, it still existed and it was there, and it still was good.

"Sure," Andrew Hunter said, "I'll talk about her. I married her eleven years ago. I was twenty-five then. She was twenty-one—about your age." There was no sign from the girl to confirm what her age was; she only sat there in the half-light of the tavern, watching him and listening.

"She had brown hair and a good figure," Stat Hunter said, "and she came from a big family in a town outside of Omaha, and she thought there wasn't anything in the world like a ballplayer. I was in the big league then, and we were living in Chicago, and she didn't like it when the ball club was out of town, but she understood. That's the thing about Marian. She understood. When Janet was born and we were hot up there in the pennant race and playing in the East and Marian was in labor for two solid days and I got that wire from the doctor, what do you think I did? Go home to be with her? Hell, no. Not Stat Hunter, the nice guy. No, I didn't even tell my manager anything was wrong. I just went out and played ball, and after the baby was born I talked to Marian on the phone long-distance, and she didn't say anything about my not having been there. The time I didn't take her to spring training, because the club suggested the players would be better off without having their wives along, she understood. I never cheated on her. So help me, I never cheated on her. But I'll tell you something." Hunter drank from his glass. "I'll tell you something. I think it would have been more of a marriage if I had. It would have meant something was wrong at home. The way it was, nothing was ever wrong at home. The baseball season's a long season. One time it was Janet's birthday and she was going to have a ghost party for her friends and I was going to be the ghost and only Janet was going to know about it, you know, so she wouldn't be scared but all the other kids would be. And the club had booked me for an Elks luncheon someplace, and I went to the luncheon and Marian's brother went over to the house and dressed up like a ghost instead of me. All the Elks were real happy to see me. When it was over, they went around telling each other, you know that Stat Hunter? What a *nice guy.*"

"So she left you?"

"Sure she left me."

"I wouldn't have."

"No?"

"No."

"Why not?"

"Because," Jo Ann said, "when you're a ballplayer's wife you accept certain things as having to be the way they are before you get married."

"It wasn't a question of that. I told you Marian understood about that."

"I don't think she really did."

"I do. It wasn't just baseball. Do you want another drink?"

"All right," Jo Ann said, "if you do. Would you like to dance with me while we're waiting? Do you like to dance? Do you have special songs you hate to hear?"

"Lay off my back," Hunter said. "Sure, I've got special songs. I've got special places, too, and certain things to eat, and certain times of day, and the things some people—some people, hell, most people—never think about one way or the other, like the way the street signs were painted in Chicago, yellow with black lettering. What are you going to do about it?"

"You feel sorry for yourself, don't you?"

"You're damn right," Hunter said. The waiter came over and he ordered another round, and then he said, "Come on. We'll dance."

She danced close to him, and they did not say much. The orchestra at the Black Widow was three pieces—sax, piano, and drums. It was all right. Hunter told himself he liked the music, and he liked the place, and he liked the girl. *Get yourself a girl,* he said to himself. *Get yourself something to come home to after the ball game. Maybe in the old days you wouldn't have thought much about anything except the game, but what about it now? Have you learned? Have you changed?* He thought about it for a while, holding the girl against him, breathing her presence, and he said to himself, *Yeah, sure. The only thing you know how to do is play ball. The only thing in the whole damn world.*

He was thinking that way, holding Jo Ann as they danced, when the big man came and cut in. Hunter had never seen him before; the stranger seemed to want to talk to Jo Ann more than to dance with her and, once the music had stopped, he brought her directly back to the table.

"I'd like to go home now," she said to Hunter. "Is that all right?"

"Sure," he said, and signaled the waiter.

He drove her home. When he stopped the car in front of her house, she said, "I suppose you wondered why. I mean, who that was and why we left."

"Is it any of my business?"

She laughed shortly. "I don't know. You can kiss me good night, Stat."

He kissed her, and the warmth and good feeling of it nearly brought tears to his eyes. Jo Ann looked at him and said, "I like you, Mr. Manager."

"I like you too," he said.

"You know where I am," she said. "Good night."

Ollie Marcus, the Philadelphia scout, was in town the next evening, in time for the game against Rome. Harry Masick pitched a seven-hitter for Stat Hunter and walked only two men. Hunter had Walt Corio at first base, moving him to fifth in the batting order and dropping Chet Maraczewski to sixth. It was nothing-nothing, and then with two out in the third inning Conway got hot and everybody got on. George Crimeau doubled.

Corio singled him home. Maraczewski flied deep to right field, and when the outfielder stumbled and dropped the ball as he started to make the catch, Corio came all the way around and Maraczewski went to third under a wild relay throw, then got up and came on home while the Rome pitcher, back of the play, was trying to find the handle on the ball. Ed Rosch walked and stole second, Oscar Johnson and Harry Masick both got topped infield hits, Joe Whittier doubled to the wrong field, Gladstone and Hunter singled and Crimeau, up for the second time, hit a home run. It totted to ten runs, all with two out, and Conway went ahead to win it 16 to 2. It was a bad baseball man who could say save some of those runs for tomorrow. Conway had won it big, and the Auburn club lost again, and now the lead was down to a game and a half with the Bears getting last place Batavia into Fairchild Park for a double-header tomorrow night, a single game Sunday night, another single game Tuesday night. Then the Bears would be on the road.

The good feeling that came with winning this one, bulwarked by the fact that with ten runs in the third inning there was no need to make any long throws from center field, left Stat Hunter in a mood of exhilaration when he got to the clubhouse. The players had it too. Corio and Whittier were talking jubilantly to each other, and Hunter, looking at them, decided to put off the talk he was going to have with the young second baseman—put it off, at least, until Marcus had left town. As for Corio, Hunter wondered why he had ever doubted him. The man was a professional. From the way he batted, the manager presumed it likely that Corio would not hit too well against good pitching. But there was not too much good pitching in the Empire League—not unless you listened to George Crimeau, who now was recounting each of his hits today as if they had been produced at the direct expense of Lefty Grove.

"That *left*hander was figurin' on blowin' ol' George *down!*" Crimeau exclaimed. "I seen him before th' game—I had my eye on *him,* never you mind! I seen him talkin' to that catcher. Put it in there right heah under ol' George's *hands,* that's what they was sayin'. Well, ol' buddies, they put it in there right heah a little too *good,* that's all. I watched that ball. I know you ain't supposed to watch no ball after you hit it, but I watched that ball. That ball was still goin' up when it left th' ball park. That right, Stat?"

"Probably still rising," Hunter said.

Ed Rosch came up to him and said, "Stat, I near fell down going around second in the seventh that time. What foot are you supposed to use to hit the bag with?"

The manager looked up. "Six of one and half dozen of the other. A lot of big leaguers use the inside foot."

"Why? Sort of to pivot on?"

"No," Hunter said. "When you're making a wide turn—that is, figuring before you get to the base that you're going to go for at least one more—you don't really turn sharply enough at any one point to need a pivot. One thing about the inside foot is that your next step will be with the outside foot, which has the effect of keeping you on an even line in the curve that you're running in. But the big thing about it is that using the inside foot you're less liable to miss the base. If you get in the habit of using the outside foot, then what you're doing is cutting the corner as fine as you can. And you might cut it a little too much. If you want to practice it, you'll probably find you're already in the habit of hitting the base with one foot regularly already. But the big thing is not to get it in your mind that you absolutely have to hit the base with a certain foot, not so you get to the point where you break stride doing it."

Joe Whittier had been listening to them. He said now, "I always use the outside foot."

"You've got some things to learn about running bases."

"You think so?"

"I know so," Hunter said. "I've been in baseball all my life, and I'm still finding out things I hadn't known before."

"Such as?" the second baseman said.

Hunter looked at him. Then he said, "Come on, Joe, that's a bush-league question."

Whittier moistened his upper lip with his tongue. "You get my girl home all right last night?"

"Yup," Hunter said. "While you were having your car fixed."

"I'll tell you about that after a while."

"I'd like to hear about it after a while."

"Then maybe I won't tell you."

"Maybe you don't have to."

"Meaning?"

Hunter shrugged. "Anything you like."

"I'll tell you what I like. I like that broad."

"You had a funny way of showing it last night."

"I had something else to do. Meanwhile, suppose you lay off of her."

"Suppose she lays off of me."

They had been fencing on the borderline, but it was up to the manager to decide whether this was the right time, and already he had decided it was not. Now he turned away and said aloud, "How many in a row now?"

"Five," said Phil Gold, the second-string catcher. "We win five straight."

Bo Walsh, the pitcher, said, "How many in a row we got to win before we can't change socks any more?"

Vagrancy Williams said, "Cain't see why you ask that. You don't change yours nohow."

"At least I wear 'em," Walsh said.

Hunter said, "Wait till one of you is pitching a no-hitter. You talk about superstitions. Wait till you see what happens then."

He could see his players gathering around him now as children might for a story teller. One of them said, "Ever see a no-hit game in the big league, Stat?"

"Three," Stat Hunter said. "One for and two against."

"What about the one for?" The question came from George Crimeau. For some reason, ol' George's experience in the major leagues had not included a no-hit game. For the same reason, none of them, not even Monk Gladstone, kidded him about it now. Instead, they listened to Stat Hunter. This was the old pro talking, and they all of them, every man in his own way, knew it.

"Well," Hunter said, "the big thing is getting to the point where you know your man's working on a no-hitter. Usually you'll go five full innings. Maybe you won't go quite that far when some fielder comes up with a real good play and then you tell yourself that would have been a hit, and then you wake up to the fact that the pitcher's going for it all."

Luis Aloya said, "Then what?"

"Then you find yourself doing just what you've been doing. If you dropped your glove in a certain place and then gave the base a kick on the way to the dugout, you make sure you do the same thing, even though you've been doing the same thing unconsciously for years. If you were sitting in the dugout with your leg up and your chin resting on your knee when you decided this might be a no-hitter, then you keep on sitting just the same way. It's superstition, sure, but you'd be surprised how it gets ahold of you. If you go eight innings with a no-hitter, and somebody gets a glove on a sure hit in the ninth, the official scorer will give him an error if he at all possibly can. If there's two out in the ninth and two strikes on the hitter and the pitcher gets the ball anywhere near the plate, the umpire will call it a strike.

"You know the story of Billy Evans and Walter Johnson? Johnson was pitching a terrific game one day against Detroit, and the last man up in the game for the Tigers was some real heavy hitter—Sam Crawford or somebody like that—and Johnson gets the third strike over, and when Evans told the story later he said it was the most perfect pitch he ever saw. But for some reason, Evans called it a ball. Umpires are human, as you can see every night out here. The next pitch comes and Crawford hits it a mile into center field, and Clyde Milan started going for it, and Evans said later he was just standing there praying for Milan to make the catch. Well, Milan went up against the wall and made a sensational catch and the game was over, and Evans started for the dressing-room. Up to this time, Johnson hadn't said a word to him. But now he walked over to him and said, 'Billy, what was wrong with that next-to-last pitch?' So Evans pulls one out of left field and says, 'What did *you* think was wrong with it.' Johnson thought for a minute and then he said, 'Might have been a little low.' "

The Conway players laughed. One of them said, "Was that a no-hit game, Stat?"

Hunter shook his head. "No, I just got to talking about umpires calling them wrong. No, about no-hitters: the big thing is, you never say a word about it in the dugout. And nobody talks to the pitcher. I've known of managers who wouldn't even give a pitcher instructions when he went up to hit because they didn't want to break the spell. One night one of you guys will throw a no-hitter, and then you'll see what I mean."

The door to the clubhouse opened and Ollie Marcus came in. He was a smallish, exceptionally round man who wore a straw hat and had a blue shirt that was open at the throat. He said hello to George Crimeau and to Vagrancy Williams and to Monk Gladstone, and came over to shake hands with Andrew Hunter.

Looking up again, he saw Walt Corio and nodded to him. Corio nodded back.

Marcus said, "Didn't I see you before?"

"Don't think so," Corio said. His voice was soft.

"Sure I did," Marcus said. "Wait a minute. Let me think."

"Did some playing in Tennessee," Corio said evenly.

"No." Marcus shook his head. "No, it wasn't there. Wait a minute. What's your name? Corio?"

Corio nodded.

"That's not the name I remember," the scout said. "Give me a minute."

"I played under another name."

"What other name?"

"I'm not telling that," Corio said. "I needed a little money and I had a couple of medals from amateur track, and if they found out I was playing ball they'd make me give the medals back. I aim to keep them."

"Oh," Marcus said. He fetched a toothpick from the breast pocket of his shirt and examined it carefully for flaws, then placed it in the corner of his mouth. "Amateur track?"

"AAU," Corio said, and headed for the shower room.

"Amateur track," Ollie Marcus said again, watching Corio go. Then he turned to Stat Hunter. "You going to have a few minutes afterward?"

"Sure," Hunter said. "Let me get dressed."

He showered and dressed quickly, and then he and Marcus went out and got in the Dodge. Marcus said, "Let's just drive around. Jeez, it's hot. Stat, what about Joe Whittier betting his money?"

"I give up," Hunter said.

"What does that mean?"

"Nothing," Hunter said, "except that everybody including President Eisenhower knows Whittier's been gambling, how much, where he lost it, why he lost it, who he lost it to, the exact amount he owes, and probably what he's figuring on doing to recoup. Me, I just found out about it last night, and then it was sort of accidental."

Marcus moved his lips and the toothpick changed sides. "Well, we wanted to give you a chance to get straightened around on the new job, and the kid's been going great out there, and we figured you'd find out about it sooner or later anyway."

"I haven't talked to him about it yet." The manager laughed without mirth. "I figured I was going to wait till you got out of town. I didn't know you knew about it."

"Nuts," Marcus said. "Well, you're going to have to do something. Exactly what, I don't know. I could kill that Kelly."

"Lester Kelly? Why?"

"He's got that new man rooming with Whittier. I wish I could remember where I know that Corio from. He hits pretty good in this league. He's been there before. I don't like it, Stat. Nothing I can put my finger on. I just don't like it. How's your little girl?"

"Janet's good," Hunter said. "I got a letter from her yesterday. She said she was going to get some kind of a surprise. Kelly said he thought it might be a pony."

"Maybe a turtle with an American flag painted on the shell," Marcus said. "I had one of them when I was a kid. It fell out of the fourth-floor window where we lived and I never did see it again. I had a funeral service for it and everything."

"Listen," the manager said, "so long as we're talking about everything, I got a young man I want you to watch tomorrow night. Pitcher named Simon North."

"Well," the scout said, "use him in the first game. I want to shake this town."

Hunter shook his head. "No," he said, "we're going to have Collins umpiring back of the plate in the second game so I have to use Bo Walsh in the first."

"Swell," Marcus said. "How's old Cross-Eyed? They got a new league, Class F, up on the Gaspé Peninsula, and they're looking for umpires."

The Batavia Colts, who had managed to win eleven of their first forty-one games, were a pleasure for the Conway Bears. Bo Walsh threw a four-hitter in the opening game, and only a double error by Joe Whittier, who goofed a ground ball and then threw it away, robbed the lefthander of a shutout. Conway won it 8 to 1. Whittier and Corio both had home runs, the former's coming with two men on.

In the stands, Ollie Marcus sat sweatingly, supplied with one pencil, one torn envelope on which to write, and twenty-four toothpicks. He liked the way Joe Whittier played ball. Marcus had his problems too. Twice in the past three years he had had a chance to sign a young star, and each time he had passed, and both players now were in the major leagues. Whittier actually was not a Marcus product, but after the Philadelphia Bears brought him up and he clicked, then the sports pages would record faithfully that the eagle eye of scout Ollie Marcus had paid off again.

Now Simon North was warming up for the second game, and Marcus sat forward in his seat, watching the young pitcher. North would be fast tonight. He would, Marcus told himself, strike out at least eight hitters.

Simon got four of them in the first two innings. He fanned the first two men he faced, got the next one on a pop-up to Oscar Johnson at short, struck out the next man, got the next one to foul out, and fanned the one after that.

In the bottom half of the second inning, meanwhile, Conway got a run. Corio singled, Maraczewski bunted him ahead, and Rosch and Johnson singled back to back for the score.

Up in the stands, Ollie Marcus nodded approval of Stat Hunter's strategy. With North pitching as well as he was, Hunter had had Maraczewski bunt, playing not for the big inning but for the lead run.

The first man up for Batavia in the third inning grounded out to Corio, unassisted. The next one hit a grounder in the same direction, but wider of the bag, and Corio let Whittier take it. The second baseman hesitated for a moment, unsure of whether it was his play, and the ball struck off the heel of his mitt and rolled on into right field. Maraczewski's throw to second was good but late.

The Conway infield hollered it up. "To go, boy, to go, way to go boy!" Out in center field Andrew Hunter peered in the uncertain glare of the lights and saw that George Crimeau was calling for one fast ball after another. North struck out the next man, and got out of the inning when the next hitter flied shallowly to Ed Rosch near the left-field line.

In the dugout, Whittier said to Hunter, "Stat, I thought Walt was going to take that ball."

Corio overheard him. "I hollered yours. What does 'yours' mean? Mine?"

"Forget it," Hunter said shortly. If it had been young Luis Aloya playing first base instead of Corio, he would have told Luis to shout it out and wave with his glove, so there would be no mistake, but there was no use in telling Corio. Corio had been around. Besides, Whittier still had been back behind the ball, and should have made the play.

North struck out for Conway. Whittier was out on a close play, short to first. Monk Gladstone walked and Stat Hunter put one down the right-field line for two bases, bringing Gladstone around to score and making it 2 to 0.

North struck out his sixth and seventh men in the top of the fourth. The other man hit back to the mound and the pitcher threw him out. Conway failed to score in its half, and in the top of the fifth, with one out, North grooved a fast ball and the Batavia hitter rammed it on a rising line out toward left-center field.

Stat Hunter had his back turned with the swing of the bat. He looked once over his shoulder, then put his head down and ran. Ahead of him, the fence loomed closer, like a curtain in the dark. Now, still going full speed and without turning he put up his gloved hand, felt the ball there, and turned his right shoulder so that the impact of going up against the fence would not jar the arm and hand that held the ball. Another foot, and he would have crashed the fence hard. This way, he caromed easily off, holding the ball up for the umpire to see.

The rising cascade of sound from the stands had more to it than mere salute for a remarkable catch. It was as if everybody in the ball park realized, for the first time and at the same moment, that it was official now—Simon North was going for a no-hitter.

Batavia had got only one semblance of a hit—the ball Whittier loused up was clearly an out, and there had been no hesitation on the part of the official scorer in tagging the second baseman with an error. No, the only good shot had been this one just now, and Stat Hunter had taken it away.

North got the next man to pop up. Hunter got a big hand from the fans back of first base as he came in to the dugout, and, reaching the dugout steps at the same time as his manager, North started to say something. But Stat Hunter moved past him without speaking and went over to the water cooler. When he finished his drink, he said, "Couple of runs, you guys. Let's go."

Conway got three. Corio tripled, Maraczewski and Rosch singled, Johnson flied deep, and North bunted Rosch to second. Hunter wanted the sacrifice with one out. He did not want his pitcher running. He left it up to Whittier, and Whittier singled out over second to bring the third run around.

Thus the Bears led 5 to 0 going into the sixth, and Stat Hunter wanted no more runs. He wanted North to pitch with as little wait in between innings as possible.

The infield pepper talk had not changed, but the way the fans roared on every pitch now it was evident something was different. North bore down. He got another strikeout. The next man tried to drag a bunt and North, showing no sign of his foot injury, came easily off the mound and threw him out.

The third hitter for Batavia in the top of the sixth hit sharply into the dirt just in front of Monk Gladstone. Gladstone pulled the toe-hop out of the dust and threw the batter out by ten feet.

Hunter, Crimeau, and Corio went down in order in the Bears' half of the sixth, and three infield flies took care of Batavia in the seventh. Another strikeout, a fly to straightaway right field, and a slow roller that Shortstop Oscar Johnson had to come in on and throw underhand, knocked out Batavia in the eighth.

Then in the top of the ninth, Simon North walked the first two men he faced. Stat Hunter called for time and came in to the mound. George Crimeau came out from behind the plate and took off his mask, and Gladstone came over from third.

"That umpire ain't givin' this boy a *break*," Crimeau said.

"Never mind that," Hunter said. "Simon, you're working these hitters too hard. Just quit worrying and throw the fast ball. We'll catch them if they hit them. That's what we're out here for. Is your fast one all right?"

"I think so," the pitcher said.

"Fastest I ever seen," George Crimeau said loyally. "Come on, now, boy, you just pitch to ol' *George.*"

"All right," Hunter said. He slapped North on the shoulder and headed back for center field.

Squinting in the lights, he saw Crimeau put down one finger. North wheeled in with the fast ball, and as he did the baserunners took off in a double steal. Crimeau shot the ball down to third base and Gladstone put it on the man for the out.

North struck the batter out with his fast ball. Now there were two out, and the next hitter was the Batavia left fielder, a right-handed batsman. He took ball one inside and low. On the next pitch he swung, a little late, and the ball traveled upward in a high arc, headed for short right-center field.

For a moment Stat Hunter lost the ball in the glare of a misdirected arc light. He flicked his sun glasses down from the underside of his visor and saw it now, and he knew there was neither loft nor strength enough in the ball to carry it far. Hunter was moving in now, patting the pocket of his mitt with his bare hand, and then he became aware of Joe Whittier, backing up on the grass, headed his way.

"I got it, Joe!" Hunter called, and kept coming. Whittier still was backing up, his glove held Indian-style on his forehead, his eyes on the ball.

The two fielders were coming together. Oscar Johnson, the shortstop, yelled out, "Stat's ball! Stat! Stat!"

Hunter was almost under it now and still Whittier came. In one final sickening moment they collided together, the manager falling away from the younger man, rolling once, ending up on his hands and knees.

Whittier had caught the ball for the final out. The place was a madhouse now. The no-hitter was in. The second baseman looked down at the manager. "You knew Marcus was in the stands. What are you trying to do, you son of a bitch?"

Still on his hands and knees, Stat Hunter looked up at Whittier. "That'll cost you twenty-five, Joe," he said evenly. "So long as you owe everybody else in town, you're going to owe me too."

In the stands, Ollie Marcus took a new toothpick and made a note with his pencil.

CHAPTER THREE
ONE AND ONE

C ONWAY RAN IT UP to thirteen straight, the winning streak, and led the Empire League now by four games.

When you went right, nothing could go wrong. Joe Whittier was hitting .386 now; he had thirteen home runs, he led the Empire League in runs scored and runs batted in, was second in the league in stolen bases. During the streak, Walt Corio had batted in more runs even than Whittier. The pitching was hot. The fielding was hotter. Monk Gladstone had started a triple play against Auburn, after catching a wicked liner with a bases-loaded, none-out situation.

Some other things went unnoticed: Stat Hunter's bad arm, Joe Whittier's bad debts, and the bad way the girl, Jo Ann, had of playing them off against each other. Each of the two men could do without her, but Whittier wanted her for the pride of it, and Hunter wanted her for the comfort.

The night before the team had left for its out-of-town swing— it was a Tuesday, three nights after Simon North's no-hitter— Hunter had seen Jo Ann. She was sitting in his car, waiting for him when he came out of the ball park.

"I thought you might be outside," Hunter said. He had been the last, as usual, to leave.

"Joe didn't see me," she said, as though the manager would want that reassurance.

"He saw you last night."

"I'm his girl," she said, and placed a hand on Hunter's knee. "Or was."

"You had him drinking last night."

"Joe's a big boy," the girl said.

"And you're a big girl. Why don't you leave him alone?"

"Jealous?"

"Cut it out," Andrew Hunter said. "You know what I mean."

"No, I don't." Jo Ann yawned and put her hands back of her head, and he saw the way it made her dress taut. "He said you weren't talking to him."

"I'm not."

"You fined him twenty-five dollars."

"I've got some news for him. He's going to pay it."

"That's what you say."

"Don't be pointless," Hunter said. "The only thing that can save that second-baseman boy friend of yours is going to be getting called up so he can get out of this town. If I tell Philadelphia he's a bad man to deal with, Philadelphia won't touch him."

"You mean his future depends on you?"

"I'd say so, more or less."

"Joe doesn't think about it that way," the girl said. "He thinks Philadelphia will call him up no matter what you say."

"He does?"

She nodded. "Besides, he says if Philadelphia doesn't call him up, some other club will. Joe says statistics speak for themselves."

"Joe has all the answers, doesn't he?"

"Yup," she said. "And you don't really know what to do about it, do you?"

Hunter smiled bitterly. She rested her hand lightly on his leg once again, above the knee this time. "Where are we going?"

"I don't know," he said. "Where did you want to go?"

"Do you want to come up to my place? I have some bourbon."

"What does Joe drink?"

"Bourbon."

"I suppose he was there last night. What do you want to do? Compare—"

She interrupted him. "Jealous. That's you. Did you—"

"Sure," he said, "and while we're on the subject, what about Corio? You're his pal too, aren't you?"

"What if I am? Maybe I've already dated him. So what? Jealous. Suspicious. Is that why your wife left you?"

"Cut it out," Hunter said. "Lay off, Jo Ann."

"All right," she said. She lighted a cigarette. "Let's don't fight, Stat."

"Let's go to the Black Widow," he said.

"All right," she said, and then: "I'm sorry."

"Okay," he said. "Okay. It was my fault too. I'm cantankerous and edgy and no good nowadays. I wish to hell I knew why. Nothing's going wrong. The club's winning one game after another. I don't know what's wrong. I just don't know."

She said quietly, "You need a woman."

"Yeah," Hunter said. "Sure."

After that, they did not talk until they were at the table in the roadhouse and had ordered their drinks. They sat over by the wall, next to another table where an old man sat by himself, and after a while Hunter looked carefully and saw it was old Jack Merced, the caretaker at Fairchild Park.

"Jack," the manager said. "Come on over here and be with us."

The old man looked up and said, " 'ey, Stat," and got up and brought his chair with him, and Hunter could see he already had had a lot to drink.

"Well," the manager said, "the whisky rebellion. Let me buy one, Jack."

"Sure," the old man said. "Sure. Good evening, Miss. Oh, look, it's Joe Whittier's girl friend, out with the manager. And you know where Whittier is now? He's—" The old man put a hand up to his eyes and then he said, "Sure, I'll have a drink with you. We'll drink a toast to Stat Hunter. Manager of the team with the winning streak. Pilot of the Conway Bears. Skipper of the *Flying Dutchman*. Captain of the *Titanic*. Bottoms up."

Hunter signaled the waiter and said, "What's the matter, Jack? Trouble?"

"Trouble?" The old man looked as if he were coming back from far away and trying to identify the word *trouble* en route. "Trouble? Me? Trouble? No." He pursed his lips and shook his head profoundly. "No, me I got no trouble. Except I'm an old man and I know too much, I got no trouble. No. Stat Hunter's got the trouble. Stat Hunter's got more trouble than he knows what to do with, and there's probably none of it his fault. And that's more trouble. Right there, that's more trouble, because it's—not—right."

Hunter looked at Jo Ann. She shook her head slightly. The old man was still talking.

"The team with the winning streak. What do you think I'm sitting here drinking for? You think I don't like the Conway Bears? You think I haven't been there year in and year out and seen them come and go and loved them all and laughed for them when they won and cried for them when they lost? Maybe the Conway Bears don't mean much. Maybe there's people right here in Conway that never heard of them, and maybe they're just a business like anything else, and if they win or lose so what?"

The waiter brought the drinks and set them down, but the old man ignored his glass. He pointed a finger at Andrew Hunter. "You're the best manager they ever had, Stat. I've seen you in action not even two months now, and I'm telling you you're the best manager they ever had. I can see that in a man. I can tell it. I've seen them come, I've seen them go. I don't know if you're the best baseball man. You may be." Merced nodded to himself, and lowered the finger. "You may be. But I know you're the best manager."

Hunter smiled and said, "Thanks, Jack. I appreciate that."

But the old man shook him off like a pitcher refusing the sign, and pointed the finger again, and now his voice had become loud. "So I'm sitting here and getting drunk because I want you to know something. I can't keep you from being hurt, because any way it turns out it's going to hurt Stat Hunter, but I'm going to tell you this now."

Merced's hand clutched his glass. "The team's rotten. It's going to go the way a ship goes down when the ocean's cold and it's the middle of the night and the waves are quiet and big and everything's black and you're all through. The club's loused up and lousy. They stink, those guys. They're dishonest men. They're rotten. They're going to go down and they're going to take you with them. They're going to take Stat Hunter with them."

Allowing for the old man's condition, having heard somewhere that old Jack Merced invariably got drunk once a season and foretold the doom of all, Andrew Hunter still could not fight off what was a wave of ice, a wave that started at the back of his neck and journeyed swiftly downward along his backbone. The manager took a drink and said, "All right, Jack. All right. Thanks. I appreciate this."

The old man nodded silently. "Now you'd better leave me alone. I'm an old man and when I drink I ought to do it by myself."

Hunter looked at him. Then he nodded at Jo Ann. She left her drink still unfinished and stood up and Hunter put his hand on the old man's shoulder and said, "All right, Jack. We'll see you."

He settled with the waiter near the door, and then he and Jo Ann went outside and got into the car.

She said, "We can drink at my place where there aren't a lot of old men making a lot of noise."

"He's not an old man making a lot of noise."

"I'm sorry, Stat. I didn't mean it to sound that way." She paused. "Oh, hell—maybe I'm strictly for the Corios of this world, the no-goods."

He said nothing, but drove to her place. Then he said, "I don't think I'm going to come in with you tonight. I wouldn't be much fun. There are things I've got on my mind."

"You didn't take him seriously?"

"No," Hunter said. "It's not just that. There are other things, and I'm tired, and I'm just not good company. It's not your fault. As soon as we get back from this next swing, we'll have a real time, you and I."

"Promise?"

"Promise," he said.

"Well, you can at least kiss me."

He kissed her there in the car, and for him it was not the same as the time before. Then he drove back alone to his own place and left the car on the street in front outside and went up to his room. He took off his coat and shirt, and after a while he went over to the little black table and took the cover off his portable typewriter and ran in a sheet of paper and began to write. He typed slowly, but he did not make mistakes.

Dear Janet,

I have been trying to think all this time what your surprise could be and I give up. You are going to have to tell me WHAT? Tomorrow morning Daddy will be on a bus going to a place called Auburn, where a lot of people live. Nearly 50,000 people. Isn't that a lot? There are some lakes around called the Finger Lakes because on a map they look like the fingers on your hand. And there are elm trees all along the streets. They have a hill there called Fort Hill where a long long time ago a tribe of Indians called the CAYUGAS used to fight other Indians. The Cayugas were very friendly to the white men when they came to build their homes in that part of the country. The name of the chief of the Cayugas was LOGAN. Isn't that a funny name for an Indian? The city of Auburn was built near a famous Indian trail that was called the GENESEE TRAIL. Also in Auburn they have a big jail where the bad men go.

Are you being a good girl and doing everything that Mommy tells you? You know that is the best way to be. I hope you will write soon and tell me all about your BIG SURPRISE!!!!

Love and kisses from,

Hunter took the letter out of the typewriter and went and got the fountain pen from the inside pocket of his suitcoat, and wrote at the bottom of the page, *Your Own Daddy.* He put several *x*'s underneath the signature, then ran an envelope into the typewriter and addressed it. He folded the letter, put it into the envelope, ran his tongue over the flap, and sealed it.

Then he realized he had no stamp, and he found himself laughing out loud, alone in his room. All that had happened in the past week came back to him, and it made him laugh. "Dumb bastard," he said to himself now, "the least thing you could have done was ask Jo Ann for a stamp."

He reflected that there was nothing to laugh about, and that made him laugh more.

Conway was winning on the road, and Stat Hunter had come to the only decision possible. He would put off a showdown with Whittier so long as the second baseman's play on the field held up. It was a moot question whether, so long as Whittier was playing this way, any manager would have the right to talk to him about the other thing beyond calling him to one side for a little fatherly advice. And Stat Hunter and Joe Whittier were not gripped by any father-and-son relationship. They spoke coolly to each other when they spoke at all. Hunter had avoided a showdown over payment of the twenty-five dollar fine by instructing Lester Kelly to hold that amount out of Whittier's next paycheck.

They were in Geneva the night they ran the winning streak to twelve. Vagrancy Williams allowed nine hits, but the Bears were hitting everything three Geneva pitchers threw, and Conway took it 9 to 4. Vagrancy Williams had talked to himself constantly throughout the game, and the infielders behind him were laughing as they listened. Williams was a doleful, funny map. Once, many years before, playing class D ball in West Virginia, he had been picked up by the cops outside the ball park while still in his uniform and held for vagrancy. While the local judge was pondering his fate, Williams had paced the courtroom floor, which had been newly laid with composition tile, and his sharp spikes took their effect. When the judge finally announced a fifteen-dollar fine, Williams borrowed two ten-dollar bills from a bailiff, who was a baseball nut, and presented them grandly to his honor. "Here," he said, "keep the change and buy yourself some new linoleum." After that, he was known as Vagrancy Williams.

Stat Hunter thought of this now as he returned to his hotel room in Geneva. He thought of it because Williams tonight had

THE ONLY GAME IN TOWN

made the Conway players laugh, and as they were laughing they were winning. Merced, the old man, had been wrong. There could be nothing wrong with a club that laughed and won at the same time.

Hunter was tired tonight, and when he let himself into his room and saw the big man lying on his bed, his first thought was that he was in the wrong room. Then he realized that it was the right room, but even now he did not ask how the man had got there.

He did not know the man, who sat up now on the bed, blinking in the light, and looked at him. The man wore a badly wrinkled seersucker suit, and he had very black hair and high cheekbones, and for some reason he made Stat Hunter think of Logan, the chief of the Cayugas.

Suddenly Stat Hunter recognized the man. He was the same one who had cut in on him when he and Jo Ann were dancing that first night at the Black Widow.

The man grunted now, and then he said, "Well. Mr. Hunter. I've been waiting for you." His voice seemed at once coarse and yet held in check, perhaps like that of a neighborhood tough who had decided to take a correspondence course in public speaking.

"Okay," Hunter said. "And who are you?"

The man swung his legs to the floor and sat on the edge of the bed. He took a handkerchief from the hip pocket of his pants and blew his nose vociferously. "Hay fever," he explained. "High pollen count. My name is Bird, like bird, tweet-tweet. I decided the best way to see you was this way."

"See me about what?"

The man named Bird blew his nose again. "Money."

"Get out of here," Hunter said.

"Gently," the man named Bird said. "I say to you, gently. Please sit down, Mr. Hunter. I'm an admirer of yours. Conway man myself. I need money—"

"Come on," Hunter said. "Get leaving."

"Money," the big man repeated again, as though the word was new to him, "because there are debts, and when there are debts they ought to be paid. Won't you sit down, Mr. Hunter, and sit facing me in that chair over there? Do you have any idea how much he owes me?"

"Who?"

"Whittier," the man said, and sneezed. "Oh, the worst thing about it is what it does to the eyes. The sinuses I can take. I can take them. But the eyes. They're always itching and smarting, and what they do to the appearance of a man just oughtn't to happen."

Andrew Hunter sat down. "How much does he owe you?"

"Who?" the other man said.

"Come on," Hunter said.

"Oh," the man named Bird said, "forgive me. I know you want to get to the point, as I do, believe me I do. It was a quick question you asked, though, and it confused me. It isn't only Whittier. There are four of your splendid young players who owe me money. My fault really, perhaps. *Neither a borrower nor a lender be; For loan oft loses both itself and friends, And borrowing dulls the edge of husbandry.* Macbeth." He smiled.

Hunter stared at him. "Four?"

The other man waved a hand. "Piddling amounts, really. Fifty dollars here, seventy-five there, a hundred and fifty over here. I'd even write them off, if I could think of some way to settle honorably with young Whittier. A fine baseball player, that lad. Remarkable future."

"All right. How much does Whittier owe you?" Stat Hunter did not want to hear the answer.

"One … ah … one … ah … ah." The other man finally sneezed. He caressed his nose at length with his handkerchief, then smiled apologetically. "One thousand six hundred and fifty dollars."

Andrew Hunter put his hands up to his face. After a while he opened his palms so they looked like blinkers on a race horse. "Gambling?"

The man named Bird looked offended. "Gambling, you say? No." He shook his head. "No, no, no. Merely borrowed money. At a small rate of interest, of course, but without any hint of usury."

"You're sure of that?"

"Certainly." The other man smiled. "There was gambling connected with it, but they—those splendid young players of yours—were the ones who did that." He spread his palms. "All I did, you might say, was to supply them with working capital."

Hunter nodded. "All right. Who, when and where?"

"Ah, details," the man named Bird said. "Details, details. I kept putting it off, saying to myself, no, they'll pay me, wait until tomorrow. *Tomorrow, and tomorrow, and tomorrow, Creeps in this petty pace from day to day To the last syllable of recorded time.* King Lear." He made a quick pass at his nose with his handkerchief. "And I would have waited longer. Believe me, Mr. Hunter, I would have waited longer, except that something— ah—came to my attention, and I wanted you to know about it, being an old, old Conway fan myself."

"Okay," Hunter said. "From the beginning."

"It isn't a pretty story," the man named Bird said. "Really, it isn't. There I was, really minding my own business in the Black Widow, night in, night out ..."

"Sure," Hunter said. "The Black Widow."

"Of course," the man named Bird said. "You've been there, I know. With the girl. A lovely girl, Jo Ann. I have a supreme interest in her. She, restores my—ah—youth. She has an unfortunate—ah—leaning toward—ah—baseball players, like yourself, sir, but I hope that in time she may outgrow this. Jo Ann and I are old friends. Dear old friends. Would it surprise you very much if

I asked her some day to be my wife? I have no wife, Mr. Hunter, and there are times …"

"Knock it off," the manager said. "What about the Black Widow?"

"Ah, yes," Bird said. "Well. You might call me one of the owners. Before we go any further, I have to explain to you that there are gambling games downstairs at the Black Widow, games of chance that are—ah—illegal under state law. I am telling you this as one friend might tell another, because you do not want it brought to public attention any more than I do. Oh, Mr. Hunter, I'm going to sneeze."

He sneezed. "To go on. Occasionally when players run out of money and desire to keep on playing, the house provides them with small amounts of additional capital, on a business-like basis, of course. We don't lend money to everyone, nor do we have a certain set amount that applies in each and every case. In the case of your splendid young baseball players, Whittier, and—ah—what's his name? Masick, and Rosch and Mara—Mara—"

Stat Hunter said tonelessly, "Maraczewski."

"That's it," Bird said. "I'll bet you thought I was going to sneeze again. It was just that I never can remember that name. Well, in their cases we were willing to go along."

"But now you're not willing any more."

"It isn't a question of willingness, Mr. Hunter. No, it's something else. That's the reason I'm here under such—ah—unusual circumstances. No, Mr. Hunter, to be forewarned is to be forearmed. You asked about gamblers. Another one of your players has been in contact with gamblers. The reason I know of this is that this player has approached the four players who owe me money. They are going to get the money to pay off their debts. Do you want to know how they are going to get the money? They are going to lose certain specified games of baseball, Mr. Hunter. Not just one game. Not enough money is bet on baseball in the cities in the Empire League to provide a big payoff on just one game, although I'd guess the amount that is bet, day in and day out, would surprise you. No, and not every game, because young men like Joe Whittier are too intent upon doing well for themselves, hoping to get the call from above." The man on the bed pointed skyward with his index finger. "I mean, of course, the major leagues. Nothing more celestial than that. No, and a young man like Joe Whittier would—ah—double-cross you or me or almost anyone, except himself. I do not think Joe Whittier would ever double-cross himself. Do you, Mr. Hunter?"

"No," Hunter said, "I don't. What's the name of the man?"

"What man?"

"The one who's putting in the fix."

"Some gambler. I don't know his name. This pollen count." Bird sniffed in misery.

"Cut it out," Hunter said. "I mean the man on my club."

"Oh, that one," the other man said. "Yes. His name is Carsi."

"There's no Carsi playing for me."

"Oh, but there is. He plays for you under another name."

"Corio?"

"I do believe that's the one."

"All right," Hunter said. Whittier, he had known about. Masick—Rosch—Maraczewski: that news had numbed him. Corio: by this time, anything figured. Yet Hunter was surprised to find himself as calm as he was, to find his mind working in such orderly channels. "Now two questions. One, why are you here? Two, how do I know you're telling the truth?"

The big man blew his nose. "To reply inversely, the answer to the second question is simple. You don't. You have, I would imagine, still some time in which to check—time, I would say without knowing too much about baseball, until it is young Mr. Masick's turn to pitch.

"As for why I am here, I have already explained to you. I want my money. I am afraid that if these young players become foolish and align themselves with gamblers that some serious consequences might indeed—ah—result. Then I should be in a position of jeopardy, indeed. Far from being enabled to collect what is due me, I might additionally find these young players, under the pressure of scandal and investigation, telling the authorities about the Black Widow. I believe there is more money involved than the small sums owed by three of the men. Carsi is a shrewd young man."

"You mean the police don't know about the Black Widow?"

"The ones who know about it, on the splendid Conway police force, have agreed, for reasons which you may imagine, not to broadcast their findings. I do not wish it to go any further."

"Suppose you never get paid? Suppose I hold a meeting and find out everything you said was true and get rid of Corio and they never throw a game? And suppose I just tell my players to forget about you?"

The large man stood up, gazed sadly down at his wrinkled suit, and wagged his finger. "Ah, Mr. Hunter. You're too honest a man to do that. I consider my visit to you here tonight an act of friendship. And besides, with the information already in my possession, a word from me could run your splendid young men out of baseball for life. Baseball is a very strait-laced business, I am told. The fix is on, Mr. Hunter. Don't you understand that? Move, Mr. Hunter. Move fast. *The time is out of joint.* Richard the Third. Act, Mr. Hunter. Forget you ever saw me, but act. Act quickly. Good night, sir."

The man named Bird smiled sadly, opened the door, and went out.

✣ ✣ ✣

What was it the old man, Merced, had said, the night he was drinking? *"They stink, those guys. They're dishonest men. They're rotten. They're going to go down and they're going to take you with them."*

When would Masick pitch? The night after tomorrow. If it rained, Stat would have that much extra time to check, to find out, to stop it before it became a reality on the ball field. It would have to be Masick the night after tomorrow. Hunter had only five pitchers, and all had been working starting turns. Tomorrow night—Stat Hunter looked at his watch and saw it was after midnight, and amended it—tonight Simon North would be pitching. So there was time. Not much time, but a little time.

Hunter picked up his telephone, and after a good while the operator answered and he put in a long-distance call to Lester Kelly in Conway.

Stat Hunter slept badly after that. He stayed around his hotel the next day and at four o'clock in the afternoon the wire came from Conway, and Hunter went over by the cigar counter in the lobby and tore open the envelope and read:

MY CONTACTS SAY YOUR INFORMATION CORRECT. COUNTING ON YOU.

KELLY.

They're dishonest men. They're rotten.

Then Andrew Hunter turned and went over to the single elevator that the hotel had, and went up to the fourth floor and walked down the corridor to room 424 and knocked on the door. There was no answer. Hunter knocked again, and then, more out of reflex than for any other reason, he tried the doorknob. The door was open.

Hunter walked inside and looked around, but there was no sign of Walt Corio. The manager turned around to leave, and as he did he noticed Corio's suitcase open on the bed with a long, legal-looking folio bound in blue paper lying on top of the clothes. Hunter went over and looked at it. It said on top:

COUNTY OF COOK, ILLINOIS
Domestic Relations Court

It was dated Chicago, two years before, and on the lefthand side, near the top, it said: *Hunter V. Hunter.*

Stat Hunter stood there and read the court record of his own divorce case.

It was all there.

... with cruelty and suspicion ...

All of it.

... and did strike her causing bodily injury ...

Not that it had been that bad. All divorce briefs were worded alike.

Or hadn't it been that bad? Maybe it had been worse. Andrew Hunter was a man all alone now. The afternoon sun came through the window of Corio's room and fell at his feet, and the dust of the room swirled and shone in the sunbeam.

It was too much, all in one day, discovering and remembering all at the same time. He had had enough baseball, Hunter had. Baseball had wrecked his life once and, directly or indirectly, would wreck it again now, as coldly and as certainly as he now stood furtively in another man's hotel room.

What good was baseball?

You hit the ball or you didn't hit the ball, you were out or safe, you won or lost, and so what? You grew old in baseball.

Too much, Andrew Hunter said to himself. *All at once and too much.*

In a sudden gesture he flung the divorce record down on the pillow of Corio's bed and went out of the room. He walked down the corridor till he found the door with the red exit bulb, and he walked down the stairs and out and then he walked the streets of Geneva, N. Y.

At seven-thirty that evening he showed up in the visitors' quarters at the Geneva park and started taking off his clothes. He said to Monk Gladstone, "Club meeting in here after the game. Tell the guys."

"Sure," Gladstone said. "What about?"

"Everything," Hunter said, and started putting on his baseball shirt.

Out on the field, he watched Simon North warming up; watched him with suspicion. *Maybe he's one of them,* his mind told him. *Maybe he's in the bag too.* Hadn't Merced, the old man, said the whole team was rotten?

And what else was it Merced had said? *"You think I don't like the Conway Bears? You think I haven't been there year in and year out and seen them come and go and loved them all and laughed for them when they won and cried for them when they lost?"*

Nuts, Stat Hunter said to himself.

He hit a home run in the top half of the first inning, and Conway was in front, 1 to 0.

The first two men made out in the bottom half of the first, and the next man hit a fly ball to Stat Hunter in center field. Hunter waited for it, had it in his glove, and then let it drop. He picked it up, fired to Oscar Johnson covering second, and the hitter was out trying to stretch the error. Hunter jogged in toward the visitors' dugout along the third-base line, and Ed Rosch met him coming in from left field.

Rosch said, "Golly, Stat."

Hunter did not look at him as they trotted toward the bench. He said, "Never saw the old man drop one before, hey, Ed?"

"Never heard of Stat Hunter dropping a fly ball."

"Just wanted to show you," Hunter said, "how to do it. How to make it look real. You know?"

The youngster did not answer him, and sat apart from him on the bench.

The Bears stayed in front by 1 to 0 till the fifth inning. Then Whittier, leading off the top of the fifth, tripled. Gladstone and Hunter both walked. George Crimeau singled home two runs and Corio hit a homer.

Conway was in front 6 to 0 now. Somewhere back of third base, a bull-necked Geneva fan yelled out, "Fixed! The game's fixed! The whole league's fixed!" His voice carried, and there was laughter throughout the stands.

Then Geneva came up for the last half of the fifth. The same loud-voiced fan shouted, "Let's go, Geneva! Let's get some hits! You going to let this guy pitch another no-hitter?"

Again, everybody heard him, and there it was. North was going for the moon again.

There was a taut, silent watchfulness among the Conway players. They hollered more than necessary. Oscar Johnson at shortstop whipped back of second base with two out in the sixth, gloved a skipping ground ball, and threw magnificently to first, where Walt Corio dug the ball grimly out of the dirt for the out. Coming in from center field, Stat Hunter said to himself, *You were going to give up on these guys. And look at them!* But it was a mixed mood he was in. He could not shake what had happened before the game.

There was one out in the eighth inning, and still North had permitted no hits. The man who was at bat now hit a fast, high-hopping grounder to the right side. Walt Corio moved over to first base to take the throw from Whittier. Whittier, moving to his left, never got to the ball. It was into the outfield for a single. Stat Hunter let Chet Maraczewski field it. He heard Maraczewski curse as he threw the ball on a line back to first base. Corio stabbed at the ball, missed, and the runner took off for second. George Crimeau, backing up the play, grabbed the ball and shot it to Johnson and the runner was cut down at second.

Either Corio or Whittier could have reached that grounder. This Hunter knew. His baseball mind told him that Corio had made the right play in covering first. Whittier, the deep man on the play, should have had it. Joe Whittier had deliberately let the ball go through. *Why?*

And Stat Hunter knew the reason for that, too. Whittier could not have North look too good. In Whittier's scheme of things, there was room for only one star on the Conway Bears. At the same time, Whittier had to maintain his excellence afield. This two-way pull was what made him untrustworthy—to the gamblers and to the team.

In the ninth, Whittier went high into the air to spear a line drive for the final out, and Conway had won its thirteenth straight game, 6 to 0 over Geneva, on the one-hit pitching of Simon North.

The players started filing through the tunnel from the dug-out to the dressing-room. Stat Hunter caught up with Corio and said, "Stay back with me for a minute, will you?"

"Sure," Corio said. "What did you want?"

The two of them, lagging behind the other players, were alone now on the wooden runway just inside the doorway to the dugout.

"Turn around," Hunter said.

Curio turned around.

"All right," Hunter said, and hit him. He hit him harder than he had ever hit anyone in his life. Corio fell back onto the wooden floorboards, reached for the railing of the runway, and, bracing himself there, slashed at Stat Hunter with his spikes. Hunter caught the foot by the ankle and landed on top of the other man. He punched him three times in the face, as hard as he could.

"That's enough," Corio said. Curiously, his voice had not changed much. "Get off of me."

Hunter hit him again. "For putting the fix on," he breathed, and hit him. "For letting Whittier louse up a no-hit game instead of taking the ball yourself," and hit him again. "For reading up on divorces and for taking a run at Jo Ann," and hit him twice more.

Then Stat Hunter got up.

Walt Corio got to his feet slowly. He took a handkerchief from his back pants pocket and began to wipe the blood from his face, slowly. His eyes were bloodied and very red. A light seemed to burn from the eyes. Corio said, "You found out, you bastard." Hunter hit him again, and Corio let himself be hit. Then he started wiping his face all over again.

"That's it," Hunter said. "You're through. You don't play baseball any more."

"I've heard that before," Corio said mildly, and it was merely an observation, not a threat, but still Hunter was surprised. This part he had not known. Had Corio actually been thrown out of baseball? The thought, with what it could mean, made Hunter stop where he was.

"I'm not through," Corio said now, his voice still quiet. "I'm not through, because if I go I take you and your ball club with me. That's number one. Number two is this: next time you decide to sandbag me in a tunnel, you better bring a knife, and you better make it a long one, just to keep things even. Because I'm going to have the longest knife you ever saw, mister, and I'm going to shove it right in that holy gut of yours. What do you think of that?"

Corio turned and walked along the runway to the clubhouse door, still holding the handkerchief to his face. Stat Hunter followed him. When the manager got inside the clubhouse, he saw that Corio had gone into the other room, where the wash basins were.

Hunter passed Simon North and said, "Sweet game, Simon."

"Thanks," North said. "You're all out of breath."

"I know it," Hunter said, and raised his voice. "You men ready for the meeting?"

Vagrancy Williams said, "Ain't we gonna get dressed first?"

"No," Hunter said.

"Well, get the new man then," Williams said, motioning in the direction of Corio in the next room.

"We don't need him," Hunter said. "Now hear this. Listen to me now, and listen real good, every damn one of you guys."

They looked at him, mostly in surprise, but they were silent, listening. They sat on the benches in front of their lockers while Stat Hunter paced the floor in the middle of the room.

"A little story," Hunter said. "A fable. Once upon a time there was a Class C baseball club. One of the players on it owed a man fifty dollars and didn't have the money to pay him. Another one of the players owed a man seventy-five dollars. Another one of the players owed a man a hundred and fifty dollars. Another one of the players owed a man one thousand six hundred and fifty dollars."

Purposely, Hunter kept from looking at any of his players. "These players had borrowed the money to gamble with, so

they didn't want to tell anybody about the money they owed."
Walt Corio had come back into the room. He was standing over
by one of the far lockers, holding his handkerchief up against
his nose. *I broke the nose,* Hunter said to himself. He went on
talking.

"A fifth player on this team came to the other four players.
This fifth player knew a different kind of gambler—a man who
bet on baseball games. This fifth player told the other four that
if they let one or two or three ball games get away from them,
they'd have enough money to pay off what they owed.

"It seemed a little drastic a thing to do to the player who
only owed fifty dollars. It seemed drastic to the one who owed
seventy-five and to the one who owed one-fifty. Maybe they
were figuring on doing more for themselves than paying back a
small debt. It didn't seem quite so drastic to the one who owed
nearly two thousand, but he had his own selfish reason for not
wanting to throw a game. He wanted to look good as much as
possible, even if it meant somebody else on the club had to look
bad."

Still Andrew Hunter was not looking at any of his players. Monk Gladstone had a cigarette, and Hunter reached over
and took it away from him and began to smoke it, still pacing
the floor. "But the fifth player, the one who was rigging the
fix, told them it wouldn't have to interfere with their winning
the pennant or the playoffs. He said he'd turn them in for
gambling if they didn't go along. He told them nobody would
ever know the difference. They could drop a ball the way I
dropped that ball in center field tonight and everybody in the
ball park would think it was an error. Did you think it was an
error, Chet?"

Now Hunter was standing in front of Maraczewski.
Maraczewski did not look up. He nodded his head, staring at

the floor. Hunter moved over and stood in front of Ed Rosch. "Ed, you told me on the field you couldn't understand it. It didn't occur to you I'd done it on purpose, did it?"

Rosch shook his head wordlessly.

"See?" Hunter said to the rest of the players. "These two boys are outfielders. Certainly they ought to know a bagged muff when they see one. But they thought it was on the up-and-up. What about you?" Hunter pointed at Joe Whittier.

Whittier looked up. "I ..."

"You what? Come on, Joe, speak up."

Whittier said quickly, "I thought it was an error," and looked away.

"See?" Hunter said. "I'll bet even the pitchers thought it was an error. How about it, Harry?"

Harry Masick nodded. He was busy with a shoelace.

"All right," Hunter said. "Now, this ball club I'm telling you about, it found out about those four players who owed money. The manager held a clubhouse meeting. You might say it was something like the meeting I'm holding now. The manager got up and, without naming the four players, he told them that the money they owed would be withheld from their salaries, a certain chunk each month, until it was paid off. The manager intended to see each of the four players separately later on to confirm that that was what they owed, and to find out if they owed anybody else anything more. Then he said this, and now I'm quoting this manager word for word:

"If a man on this club touches a deck of cards or a pair of dice or the skin on a roulette table, he is off this club and his case goes to the president of the minor leagues with the manager's own recommendation for extreme discipline. If a man on this club so much as says hello to a gambler, he is off this club and it goes to the president at Columbus the same way."

Hunter let the cigarette fall to the floor and ground it black with his heel. "As for the other player, the one who owed no money but who lined it up to go off the low board with the four players who did, this manager decided to deal with him privately. He did this for one reason. Because the club had been winning, and for that reason the manager saw no reason to penalize the rest of the players." Was that the ghost of a smile on the face, the battered face, of Walt Corio? Hunter licked his lips. "To bring that situation to a head by itself would have brought down some kind of penalty on the club as a whole. The manager did not think this was right. However, he did deal privately with this player. And this player never forgot it."

Stat Hunter paced the floor in silence. Then he looked around and snapped, "That's all."

Nobody moved.

"That's it," Hunter said. "You've had it. Get to putting your clothes on so we can all go home and get some sleep. You played a good game of ball out there tonight."

There was a knock on the door. Bill O'Brien, nearest the door, opened it, and, looking out, Stat Hunter saw that it was one of the Geneva sports writers.

"This is private," Hunter said.

"This isn't," the writer said, and threw a newspaper on the floor at the manager's feet. It was a copy of the next morning's Syracuse paper. There was a headline about Russia and the UN, and underneath there was another eight-column banner, in italics, and this one said:

Reveal Banned Player in E.L.

E.L. was short for Empire League. Stat Hunter picked it up, looked at it; then he said, "All right. Now get this."

He read the headline aloud, and then the story.

> "CONWAY, N. Y., July 2—*The Conway Times disclosed in a copyrighted story tonight that Walt Corio, star first baseman for the first-place Conway Bears of the Empire League, was banned from baseball in 1946 in a betting scandal in Texas, where he was playing organized ball under the name of Carsi.*"

Hunter read the whole story to them. Nowhere in the story was there any mention of the money owed the Black Widow by Whittier, Masick, Maraczewski, and Rosch. Nowhere was there any mention of the attempt through Corio to rig games.

Stat Hunter was grateful for this. When he was through reading the story, he looked directly at Walt Corio.

Corio lowered the handkerchief from his face and looked back. There still was the shadow of a grotesque smile on his reddened, injured face.

Hunter was not the only man in the room who was staring at Corio. Now Corio took a step forward.

"I'm sorry," he said softly, "that that came out. Up to now, I played as good as I knew how. I'll tell you the four players Stat was talking about. They were Masick, Whittier, Rosch, and Chet here. To save his own skin, one of them found out about me and gave the story to the papers. That's what I think. So now I'm going to tell the papers *my* story. About how the great Conway Bears gambled away money they didn't have while the manager stood by and did nothing about it."

Now the players looked at Stat Hunter. The manager took off his cap and wiped his brow with his sleeve. Then he said, "No, you won't." His voice was low. "If you tell what you threaten to tell, then I'll give out the story about how you tried to bribe my ballplayers. Those kids will talk. This isn't Texas and it isn't 1946. You don't get banned from baseball this time. You go to jail. You've committed a felony. Get out of here, get out of town, and get out of this state as fast as those lousy yellow legs will carry you. And if you want, you can take my divorce papers with you."

CHAPTER FOUR
TWO AND ONE

THE HEADQUARTERS of the Empire League of Professional Baseball Clubs is in Waterloo, New York. The Empire League consists of franchises in Conway, Rome, Geneva, Auburn, Batavia, and Waterloo, and the only reason the league office is in Waterloo is that Ironton Farney Kane, president of the league, does business there as executive director of a bank. Other cities in the league are bigger than Waterloo, but other cities in the league do not have Ironton Farney Kane.

Stat Hunter had never met Kane. When Conway opened at home, Kane was throwing out the first ball at Batavia, and when Conway was the visiting team for a secondary opener at Rome, Kane was throwing out the first ball at Geneva.

He had heard stories about him though. Ironton Farney Kane was a man steeped in righteousness and Biblical quotations. Ironton Farney Kane was opposed to sin.

In Conway, the offices of the Bears, who did not run a bank, were in a bank building. In Waterloo, the offices of Ironton Farney Kane, who ran a bank, were in one of the hotels. Kane maintained a suite there. For a secretary, he had a little old lady who looked more like an owl than most owls. Even in July, she wore a little jacket or a sweater.

Now it was the second morning following the news about Corio. Last night, with Harry Masick pitching, the Conway

Bears had lost to Geneva 14 to 3. The Bears had made six errors, two by Oscar Johnson at shortstop, one each by Hunter, Whittier, Rosch, and Luis Aloya, who was back at first base. Never had a team looked worse. Never was a game more honest.

By royal command, Hunter and Lester Kelly, the general manager of the Bears, sat now in the anteroom in the offices of Ironton Farney Kane. Outside in the corridor newspapermen and photographers smoked cigarettes and examined some of the cameramen's non-publishable stills.

"Mr. Kane," said the little lady secretary who looked like an owl, "is conferring at the moment. He will see you gentlemen very anon."

Hunter said, "Very anon?"

"Or sooner," the secretary said. "Would you two gentlemen desire to share a copy of Fortune magazine? I have last month's."

Hunter and Kelly declined.

They sat there for the better part of an hour. Then three small lights alongside the secretary's telephone went on simultaneously.

"You two gentlemen," she said. "You can go in now."

Hunter and Kelly stood up and went into the inside room. Kelly had warned his manager to be prepared for anything. Hunter still was not prepared.

Ironton Farney Kane was lying on the couch in the room. He was a reed-like, excessively puritan-looking man of perhaps sixty-five years of age. The skin of his face, down alongside the jaw and toward the neck, was loose but not tough; it was soft and almost unwrinkled. His mouth was a thin straight line. An artist would have drawn it with a pencil and ruler.

Ironton Farney Kane was lying on his back on the couch. He wore rimless eyeglasses but his eyes were closed. He had on a white shirt, with *IFK* monogrammed in small but indubitably purple braid upon the breast pocket.

"Are the transgressors here?" The eyes remained closed.

Hunter looked at Kelly. Kelly's eyebrows went up hopelessly and came down again.

"I say, the transgressors, are you here?"

"Yes, sir," Lester Kelly said. "I'm Kelly, sir, and this is Stat Hunter."

"How do you do?" Hunter said.

"What's your first name, Hunter?"

"Andrew, sir."

"Never forget it."

"No, sir."

"Sit down," Kane said. They sat down, waiting for him to open his eyes or move. He did neither. After a time he said, "How many games did Corio play for your team? Ten. Right?"

Kelly said, "That's right, Mr. Kane. It was ten."

"I'm ordering all ten games forfeit," Ironton Farney Kane said. "Do you understand that?"

Stat Hunter leaned forward. "I have to say I don't like that, Mr. Kane. We won all ten games and there was nothing dishonest about those games."

"You employed a man who had been banned from baseball for life. This man helped you win those games. You say there was nothing dishonest?"

"I say the games shouldn't be forfeited," Hunter said. "We didn't know about Corio."

"Be not rash with thy mouth," the president of the Empire League said suddenly, "and let not thine heart be hasty to utter any thing before God."

Hunter and Kelly looked at each other. The man on the couch still had not moved.

There was silence in the room for a time, and then Kane said, "Who hired Corio?"

Kelly said, "I did."

"Why?"

"He came to me recommended."

"By whom?"

"A man named Baumer who is in a factory that makes gears in Herkimer, and Corio used to work at this factory and played on the factory team there."

This time, I. F. Kane hardly waited for the other man to stop speaking. "You realize," he said, "that everything that is being said in this room is being tape-recorded?"

Again, Kelly and Hunter were silent, and after another period of time, Ironton Farney Kane said, "Suffer not thy mouth to cause thy flesh to sin."

The room fell quiet once again. Then the president of the Empire League began to drum on the side of the couch with his fingers, and the two other men realized he was singing. He sang in a positive, reedy voice:

"Oh, we're leavin' for the Promis' Lan'
Leavin' for the Promis' Lan'
Keep that drivin' wheel a-rollin', rollin' …"

He finished the refrain and his voice continued in its nasal, sing-song way, so that for a moment neither Hunter nor Kelly realized that he was no longer singing, but talking to them.

"The individual baseball club has the responsibility of checking on its men."

Kelly said, "We hadn't put his contract through yet. We were going to wait till the team got back to Conway."

"Funny way to do business," Kane said. "Funny way."

"Yes, sir," Kelly said.

"How do you know he wasn't losing games for you?"

Hunter and Kelly looked at each other. Then the manager said, "We figure it wasn't too likely that he lost games for us because we didn't lose any games."

"You lost last night."

"Corio didn't play for us last night, sir."

"Retribution," the man on the couch said. "A time to get, and a time to lose; a time to keep, and a time to cast away."

"Yes, sir," Stat Hunter said.

"You did not lose, therefore I shall not order these games forfeit. You played to win. I have your word for this. Therefore my decision is as follows, and will be announced today. The ten games in which Corio played for Conway are now wiped off the books. They will be rescheduled. All the individual records and statistics for each side in each game are hereby void. They do not exist."

Ironton Farney Kane began to sing again. After the first couple of bars he said, "That is all today. The transgressors will please depart."

Kelly and Hunter looked at each other one more time. The president of the Empire League, lying there on the couch, still had not opened his eyes.

"On your way out," he said, "ask Miss Fletcher to have the newspapermen come in."

Stat Hunter held another clubhouse meeting that night. He told his players what had happened, what Kane had said.

"Now to repeat what I said night before last," he said. "Nobody on this club touches a deck of cards or a pair of dice. Nobody on this club so much as looks at a gambler. Have we got that? Does anybody want to ask anything?"

Joe Whittier said, "What the hell."

Hunter looked at him. "What does that mean?"

"Why didn't you let him forfeit the games when he wanted to?"

Monk Gladstone said, "Hell, Joe, that way they take ten wins off the standings and we've got ten losses instead. What sense does that make?"

"We've got ten wins off the standings anyway," Whittier said.

"Sure," Art Vincent, the pitcher, said, "but we've got a chance to win them back. I know why Joe's mad. Joe's mad because he was hitting good while we were on the win streak. If the games had been forfeited, the individual records still would have stood. This way they're all wiped out."

Oscar Johnson said to Whittier, "Blame your pal Corio for taking your batting average away from you."

"I'm not worried about my batting average," Whittier said. "I'm worried about some of the other guys. What about Simon North? The guy's had a no-hit game taken away from him."

Chet Maraczewski said, "Simon's probably used to that by now. You took one away from him the other night."

"What do you mean by that?"

"You know what I mean by that. Anything you want to do about it is all right."

Whittier sprang, and it took three of them to get the two players apart. But Andrew Hunter, standing there and looking at their faces, knew that Whittier's words had cut. When you won ten games in a row, everybody had to be going good. They would not be human if they did not think about their personal records, and it did not augur well. Shorn of ten victories, Conway now was back in second place—and only one game ahead of Waterloo in third.

They came into Waterloo and Waterloo took four straight.

By the time they got back to Conway, they were back deep in third place.

Stat Hunter had not played in the major leagues for sixteen years without knowing what a slump was. It was something that hit you, and there was no telling why. It happened to bad clubs, but it happened with equal frequency, considering relative abilities, to good ones. The 1953 New York Yankees had won eighteen straight, then turned around and lost nine in a row. That had been a slump the Yankees could afford. This was a slump the Conway Bears could not.

Still you did not know what to do. One day of summer heat succeeded another, and this had become the worst kind of slump—a slump where you did not lose night in and night out, but occasionally won a game (though only occasionally), thus making it even more unlikely that you could find out what was wrong.

Stat Hunter rigged his line-up. He put Bill O'Brien in for Johnson, put Johnson back in and put O'Brien in left field in place of Rosch. He rested Monk Gladstone one game, Chet Maraczewski the next. He and Joe Whittier were the only two Conway players who were in the lineup every night, and that was because it had to be that way. The bench could not take either one of them out of there.

In a game against Rome—the first of the rescheduled games to fill in for the ten that had been thrown out—Bo Walsh was struck on the pitching hand by a line drive that broke his wrist.

Hunter's report to Philadelphia that night was accompanied by a brief addendum: *We're all out of lefthanders.*

The Conway Bears lost seventeen out of twenty-one games. Hunter got a note from Ollie Marcus:

Stat—
  Go find yourself a lefthander someplace. Kindly check major league standings. Phila in worse trouble than you.
                                                              O.M.

Tomorrow league-leading Auburn would be in for five games in four nights.

"The trouble is," Hunter said to Arnold Margolies, the sports editor, "nobody on this club knows how to come down again."

Margolies it was who had broken the story about Corio. He had not told Hunter where he got the story, and Hunter had not asked, although he sensed it might have been the old caretaker, Jack Merced.

Now, today, it was a Monday—an off day—and in the late afternoon, Hunter and Margolies were having a beer in the Olde Tavern downtown while Archie, the bartender, sang to himself and watched television.

"What do you mean?" Margolies said. "What do you mean, nobody knows how to come down again?"

"Old story," Hunter said. "When Smead Jolley was playing for the Red Sox they had an incline in the ground just in front of the outfield fence and Jolley was always falling over his feet trying to go up the slant. So they worked on him for weeks until he could do it, and the first ball hit out there he messed it up. And he's mad as a hen when he gets to the bench. 'You taught me to go up the hill,' he said, 'but nobody ever taught me how to come down again.' "

Margolies smiled. "What's the use anyway? Get going good and they'll take Whittier away from you. You know the way the Philadelphia club's been going? And I'll tell you something funny, Stat. With all the other minor-league clubs they've got between here and the majors, there isn't one that's got a stickout guy like Whittier. Maybe you don't like young Joe and maybe I don't like young Joe, but he's a ballplayer, and a real one."

"He could be," Hunter said.

"For my money he is now. Even money says he's in Philly before the season's over, and odds-on they don't wait for the Empire League play-offs."

"If we make the play-offs."

"You'll make the play-offs. You know why? Because as bad as you are, there's two clubs worse. Batavia and Rome."

"I've done everything I know how," Hunter said. "I've done everything, Arnold. I've given them extra practice and I've told them to take the day off. I taught them a real slick pick-off play the other day, figuring if it worked that would be the thing that would make them realize they still had class. They practiced it till they had it down so they could do it in their sleep. The first game after that, in the very first inning, like it was an act, the other club set it up for them. They timed it perfectly. So what happens? Ol' George throws the ball into right field."

"Tell me something," Margolies said. "Strictly over this bar, and not for print. Has there been any dissension?"

Hunter laughed shortly. "Sure. Over this bar, under this bar, any way you want to slice it. Dissension? Two nights ago one of them slugged Joe Whittier."

"Hell," Margolies said, "that's not dissension. Everybody slugs Whittier."

"Let me finish," the manager said. "You know who hit him? Vincent."

"Art Vincent?"

Stat Hunter nodded vehemently. "A music teacher, for God's sake. That's how bad it is."

Margolies said to the bartender, "Archie, give us two more."

"Yes, sir, gentlemen," Archie said. "Did you want me to see if I could get the Brooklyn game on television?"

"Hell, no," Andrew Hunter said.

"That's the way it goes," Archie the bartender said. "Somebody wins, somebody loses." He reached into the cooler for the beer. "Whatever happened to that fellow Corio? Came in here first day he was in town. Took one look at him, I did, and said to myself, that one's a wrong one, that one is. Archie, I said to myself, don't give that one the time of day."

"He left town," Stat Hunter said.

"Went west," Margolies said.

"Farther west the better," Archie said.

Margolies turned sideways on his stool, hoping his shoulder would indicate to Archie that his presence was not required in the conversation. After a while Archie went down to the other end of the bar and began singing to himself again, and Margolies said, "Stat, let me tell you something. I think you've done a good job with this club. When you showed up in town, I didn't know whether I liked you or not. You were a guy who snapped at other people from time to time, and you were new as a manager and you were inclined to be a little—what's the word?—pedantic with your ballplayers. I thought so, anyway.

"But by God, you're all right. Losing ball games is nothing. You stuck with your kids and you pulled them through the worst kind of a situation, and win or lose, they're better ballplayers today than they were when the season began. That's the test, Stat. That's how you tell."

Hunter said nothing for a while. He turned his glass of beer slowly in his hands. "All right," he said at last. "We don't have anybody playing a violin in the background, but it seems to be lovemaking time anyway, so I want to tell you two things. One, I'll be grateful to you all my life for digging up that story. It took care of Corio and straightened out my ball club. No, I know it was your business to get it if you could and you would have done it whether I liked it or not. I'm just grateful, that's all.

"Number two is this, and this *is* over this bar. I'm just telling you this because it's the kind of thing I wanted to say to somebody, and I don't know who else I'd tell. That night in Geneva—that sounds like a song title—all right, that night in Geneva, before the game, after I'd found out about the players being in debt and Corio going to them, I went out from the hotel and walked the streets till it was almost game time. You want to know something? It took a miracle for me to walk in that ball park that night. I was through with baseball, Arnold. I was sick and tired and upset and disillusioned and hopeless."

"And lonely," Margolies said.

"And lonely," Stat Hunter said.

They said nothing for a while; only sat there and drank their beer. Then Margolies said, "What made you decide to go through with it?"

Hunter put his glass down and looked far away. "I don't know," he said slowly. "I just don't know."

Margolies watched him. "I do," he said.

"Oh?" Hunter said.

"Sure," Margolies said. "Fellow gets taken in a crap game and a guy says to him, 'Didn't you know the game was crooked?' and the first fellow says, 'Sure, but it's the only game in town.' "

Andrew Hunter sat alone in his room that night, figuring it out. In his mind's eye, he saw his players pass in review, one by one:

Whittier—still hitting well but going after bad balls now; pressing to get his average back up there; pressing in the field, too; hurrying his throws.

Gladstone—dependable, but still Monk Gladstone; he hits best when the team is hitting.

Me—trying to do everything at once and doing not much of anything; how do you snap out of that?

Crimeau—tired.

Gold—not as good as a tired Crimeau.

Maraczewski—cost us two games with his baserunning alone.

Aloya—good field no hit.

Rosch—acting like a penitent monk because he went fifty bucks in the hole; no spirit at all.

Johnson—can make any play in the book at short; isn't making them.

Vincent—can win only with a winner.

Williams—tired.

Walsh—hurt.

North—best young pitcher in the league; can't win without support.

Masick—could be the best pitcher in baseball if the plate was low and outside.

O'Brien—still Class D.

Hunter reviewed his men once again, and then he found himself wondering how this team had managed to win thirteen straight. Had Corio made that difference? He did not want to believe this, and in truth it did not make sense, for Conway had been a winning ball club before Corio came to town.

There was a knock on his door, and when he went to answer it he saw it was Jo Ann.

"Can I come in?"

She wore the same sleeveless summer dress she had worn the first night he had taken her out. "What happened, Stat? You were supposed to be in touch with me when the team got back."

"Come on in," he said. "A few things came up." He gestured to the armchair and she sat down, her dress running up above the knee when she crossed her legs. Hunter closed the door. "We had a little trouble. It was in the papers. In addition to this I suddenly find myself unable to get runs across the plate. I can't even get a long fly ball out of this club."

"I suppose that's important," Jo Ann said.

"It's my living," Stat Hunter said.

"Well," she said, "you're still human."

"What about Whittier?"

"What about him?"

"You supposed to be his girl or not?"

"What difference does it make?"

"He's human too," Stat Hunter said. "What I'm trying to do is get him to play his kind of baseball again. You don't understand this, so I'll keep on talking anyway. There's no future for you with me or me with you because whatever it is between us is something you worry about and I don't. I like you too much to start making love to you. If I sound like a cowboy in a western movie who loves his horse more than he loves the girl, I'm sorry. When did you see Whittier last?"

Jo Ann blinked. "Three nights ago."

"You like him?"

"I don't know," the girl said. "Yes, I like him. Sure I like him. He asked me to marry him."

"Going to?"

"I don't know. Maybe. Some day."

"What about that guy Bird out at the Black Widow? You going to marry him too?"

"What did he tell you?"

"Not a hell of a lot," Hunter said. "Just that he and you were old friends. I figured the rest out for myself. That night he talked to you when we were dancing, and we had to leave right after that—some of the players must have been downstairs shooting dice. Right?"

Jo Ann's voice was almost toneless. "He won't leave me alone. I thought he'd leave me alone. That's why I sent him to see you."

"*You* sent him?"

She nodded. "I thought if he could get back the money they owed him, then he'd leave me alone. I knew enough from Corio and Whittier to know what was going to happen."

"I don't get it," Hunter said. "If you knew it, why didn't you tell me? I thought we were big buddies. I even smacked Corio one time for you."

"You did?" she said. "Now he's gone, too, and I didn't want him to go. No." She squared her shoulders. "I didn't tell you because I didn't want to upset you."

Hunter almost laughed. "You make no sense at all."

"Don't I?" She ran her tongue over her lips.

Hunter went over and bent over her with his arms on the chair, so his face was close to hers. "At the age of thirty-seven," he said, "the one thing I don't want in this world is any more complications. I know you like to feel that you're desired and desirable, and believe me you're both. You have to count me out of this. It's no good. We're just not going to make it."

Her gaze was steady, and her voice was cool. "Why don't you cut this out?" Her voice aped his. "Complications. I can't even get a long fly ball. I sound like a cowboy who loves his horse more than the girl. Stop it, Stat. Why don't you just say you're still in love with your wife?"

He stepped back. "Okay," he said. "Is there some place I can take you now in the car?"

She stood up and nodded her head. "Over to Joe's place. What do you think of that?"

"Whittier's?"

"Yes," she said.

He thought for a moment. Then he said, "All right. Come on."

⚜ ⚜ ⚜

It was a beautiful night for baseball, and the crowd at Fairchild Park, every man, woman, and child, totaled no more than three hundred. League-leading Auburn was in town, else the attendance would have totaled perhaps one hundred and fifty.

Joe Whittier came up to Hunter at the batting cage before the game. "I see you voted to give me my girl back. Many thanks."

"You flatter me," the manager said. "I never had her to give." He moved away from the other man. Over by the dugout steps, Chet Maraczewski and Luis Aloya were talking. Maraczewski looked up as the manager approached and said, "Stat, Luis and I are going to work that play where I throw back to first after the man singles to right field."

"Good," Hunter said. "Maybe we can demoralize somebody else for a change." He went on up the right-field line to take a look at two new lefthanders Lester Kelly had found someplace. They had nothing.

Back in the dugout, Hunter put a hand on Simon North's shoulder as the young pitcher went out to warm up. "I've got to come back with you Friday night, Simon. And maybe you'll be pitching an inning or so of relief in between now and then."

"All right," North said.

"But listen," Hunter said. "I want you to be absolutely honest with me. If the arm doesn't feel like it, don't pitch. Don't throw a ball if it's going to tire you. You've got a future in baseball, and what happens to your arm now is a lot more important than what happens to the Conway Bears. If you think that sounds funny coming from the manager, think of it over the long haul. Suppose I had you racked up with a sore arm for the play-offs."

The young pitcher smiled, pleased. "All right, Stat. Thanks."

Cross-Eyed Collins, umpiring back of the plate, hollered, "Pay bah!" and the Conway Bears went trotting out onto the field. The greetings from the stands were sour.

"All right, boys! All together! Let's lose another!"

"Get Corio back! Let's win 'em fixed!"

"We got Auburn in the runs pool!"

They went scorelessly to the top of the fourth. Then the first man up for Auburn singled to right field. Maraczewski waited for the ball, watching the runner as he did so, and Stat Hunter knew Chet was going to try the throw back to first. But he was too intent. The ball went through his legs and rolled to the wall, the hitter going to third.

"That's all right," Hunter said hopelessly to his right fielder. The next man singled through the right side and Auburn was in front 1 to 0. The next one lifted a shallow fly ball to straightaway center field. The man who hit the ball was the Auburn catcher, a squat, rotund individual known as the slowest man in the Empire League. Stat Hunter got under his fly ball, but instead of catching the ball he trapped it and then shot it to Johnson covering second for a force play on the fast runner who had been on first base.

There was some applause from the stands, but it had a sarcastic ring. North walked the next man, and the next one bunted. It was not a try for a sacrifice. It was a drag to the right side. Conway had been gumming this kind of play up with regularity during the slump.

Aloya had no play for the ball, but North, coming off the mound, reached it on a low hop and shoveled it to Aloya at first for a close out. Aloya and the hitter collided momentarily, and the first baseman danced away in foul territory. Then suddenly, he rifled the ball across the infield to Gladstone at third base. The lumbering Auburn catcher, off and running with the bunt, had over-turned third base. Watching the play unfold, Stat

Hunter felt a surge of pride. Aloya, on his own, had taken the over-turn play Maraczewski wanted to pull and converted it to fit the situation. In the major leagues it did not happen often because baserunners were on the watch for it. But in Class C it was something.

The Auburn catcher tried to get back to third hands first, and Gladstone put the ball on him. The play belonged to Cross-Eyed Collins back of the plate, for the base umpire had been involved in the out at first. And Collins, coming up the third-base line with his mask in his hand, put his palms down, signaling the man was safe.

Gladstone and Crimeau were screaming at the umpire, and for a change the crowd backed the Bears. Collins turned his back and started walking out toward left field. Then he looked back and saw Stat Hunter charging him.

"Easy, Stat," the umpire said. Neither he nor anyone else there had ever seen Hunter like this.

Crimeau and Gladstone followed their manager, and the three of them encircled the umpire out along the left-field line like a great carnivorous sea-plant.

"I'm talking to the third baseman about this," Collins snapped.

"He was out!" Gladstone said. "He was out this much! You were up the line from the play!"

"I'm talking to you," Collins said to him.

"You didn't even see th' *play!*" Crimeau yelled.

"I'll talk to the third baseman," Collins said.

"You'll talk to the manager," Hunter said. "You'll talk to me." The manager had his hands on his hips, his face not an inch from the face of the umpire. Stat Hunter's features were set; his voice was controlled but rapid. "You want that extra three hundred to work through the whole play-off set and you figure this club's got the best chance so you're giving 'em to them, aren't you? Even when you're not in a position to make the call, you're letting 'em have the close ones. Only you blew this one, Cross-Eyed, because it wasn't close. There was that much daylight in there and if a photographer got that one you'll be famous tomorrow, because your name'll be on every sports page from here to Honolulu. There'll be a picture of the play at third with the man out and the umpire's not only calling it wrong, he's not even in the picture." Neither his teammates nor the umpire had ever heard Hunter talk so fast. "I can forgive judgment, Cross-Eyed, but when an umpire's not alert then it's something else. I'm not protesting this. I'm sending it direct to that skinny old guy in Waterloo who lies on the couch with his eyes closed and sings to himself and quotes the Bible. I'm going to let the president of the league know what kind of umpires he's got. I'm fed up with this. The minute a ball club loses a game you've got to go and jump on them, you guys. You can't stand being with anything but a winner."

"Don't you call me Cross-Eyed," Cross-Eyed Collins said. "I'm pulling a watch on you."

"Here," Hunter said, "take mine. You're taking every other goddam thing away from us. You can pull watches till you're up to your crotch in watches and that still won't make that man safe. It still won't put you in a place to make the call, either. You stink, Cross-Eyed."

"Gay out!" Cross-Eyed Collins screamed. He swung his right arm like a creaky boxer and wound up with his thumb pointing to the Conway dugout. "Gay out of here!"

George Crimeau said, "*Listen,* 'Cross-Eye'," and Collins turned on him.

"And you!" he yelled. "And you!"—pointing to Gladstone. "Gay out all o' y'!"

"This goes right to the president," Hunter said. "I mean that. This is not just an argument on a ball field. This is more than just a judgment call. I mean it, Cross-Eyed. Right up to Waterloo."

Cross-Eyed Collins's face was an unbelievable shade of red. "Out o' here! Out o' here!"

Hunter and Crimeau and Gladstone went. Phil Gold went in to catch, Bill O'Brien went to third base, and Harry Masick, the pitcher, went out to left field with Ed Rosch moving over to take Hunter's place in center.

Old Jack Merced, the caretaker, came into the clubhouse behind the three banished players. "Stat," he said, "I was proud of you out there. Every man on the club was proud of you."

Gladstone said, "Who'd you tell to run the team?"

"Bo Walsh," Hunter said. "The hell with it."

Periodic bulletins, brought by different players from the bench, kept Hunter posted on what was going on outside. But he did not really believe it until, with the game over, he walked out to the dugout and squinted at the scoreboard on the outfield fence:

VIS.	0 0 0 1 1 0 1 1 0	4 4 2	
CNWY.	0 0 0 0 0 3 7 5	15 15 5	

"Stat," Monk Gladstone said, "believe me when I tell you one thing. That was the ball game to win."

"I'm thinking of making Bo Walsh manager," Hunter said, but he was as delighted as the rest of them. It had been like the time, years ago, in Chicago, when the big-league club had lost twelve straight and then in one game they had thrown out two runners trying to score and another two going in to third base and won it 2 to 1. It had been a totally different situation from the situation here in Conway tonight, but the feeling was the identical feeling. You did not know where it came from but you knew it was there.

"They're out of it," Hunter said to Arnold Margolies. "They snapped it. Now they're all right."

"How do you know?"

"I don't know how I know. I just know."

The next morning's paper carried a four-column picture on the front page. It was a picture of the play at third base. From the camera angle, at least, the runner was clearly out. The head caption said: *What's Wrong With This Picture?* Then it went ahead, in the eight-point type beneath the cut, to explain the whereabouts of Cross-Eyed Collins. One of the services picked up the picture and it was widely circulated. A lot of papers used it. The paper in Waterloo ran its caption in French: *"Ou Est l'Umpire?"*

Before the game that night, Cross-Eyed Collins came up to Stat Hunter and said, "What did you tell Kane?"

"Nothing," Hunter said.

"Well," Collins said, "Ironton Farney Kane hath—I mean, has—instructed me to apologize to you. I apologize. He sang to me over the telephone."

"Never mind," Hunter said.

The Bears beat Auburn 6 to 2 back of Harry Masick that Wednesday night. Thursday, Vincent won the twilight game 7 to 6 with Masick in two innings of relief and Vagrancy Williams pitched a two-hit game while the Bears were winning the second one 6 to 1.

The package came before Friday night's game. Jack Merced brought it in to Hunter while the manager was sitting in front of his locker. Stat Hunter unwrapped it and saw it was an ash tray, made of clay. On one side of the rim it said in the clay, spelled out: DADDY. Across on the other side it said: JANET. One of the grooves where the cigarette would go had been split in transit, so that now a hunk of clay came away in Hunter's hand, gray and powdery beneath the gay red paint of the exterior.

There was no note or card with it—as, indeed, there did not have to be. Hunter put the separated piece, what was left of it, carefully back in place, and put the ash tray back in the box and put the box on the top shelf of his locker. For a while, he sat there thinking, with his leg flexed up on the bench and his fingers interlocked around it just below the knee. Once, pride had been his ally, had been something that was always with him, something with which he could explain almost anything except a bad throw or a missed sign. Now he did not have it and he did not miss it.

He called Merced over and said, "Jack, are there any Western Union blanks around?"

The old man thought for a moment, and then he said, "No, but they've got Western Union in the press box upstairs and I could take it up. They can send it from there."

"All right," Hunter said. "Where's a pencil and paper? Tell them to charge me for this." He got the pencil and paper and addressed the telegram to his wife and wrote:

PLEASE SEND ANY NEW SNAPSHOTS YOU HAVE OF YOU
AND JANET. LOVE,

STAT

A month before, he would have added a line—EVERYTHING FINE HERE. A month before that, he would not have sent the telegram at all.

Simon North walked by while Hunter was handing the folded message to Jack Merced and the manager said, "You going to be all right tonight?"

"Sure," North said. "I feel fine."

"Don't say that unless you mean it."

"I mean it. I feel fine. I'm a big boy. I weighed a hundred and eighty yesterday."

"How tall are you?" Hunter asked. "Six-one?"

"And a half," North said.

"That much," the manager said, half to himself, and watched the young pitcher move away. The clubhouse door opened and Joe Whittier came in. Hunter nodded to him, but Whittier returned no recognition.

He's still sore, Stat Hunter informed himself. Then he thought, *The hell with it. One of these days he'll jump out of here. And when he jumps, it'll be all the way to the big league. He's good enough to make it. He needs two seasons more downstairs, maybe in A or triple-A ball, but he's too good for this league and he just might make it in the majors. Besides, Philadelphia's got to have something.*

Philadelphia, figured for third place and a good shot at the top, was in sixth place in the big league. The big Bears needed help at second base, and all through their farm system there was no second baseman to equal Joe Whittier.

Auburn and Waterloo were tied for the league lead now, with Conway a not-too-distant third, and tonight there was a crowd of at least six hundred in Fairchild Park. Swinging the way fans swing, they were solidly back of the Bears once again. They began to roar and chant as Simon North struck out the first four men he faced.

In the last half of the second inning, Maraczewski got on when the Auburn shortstop gummed up his ground ball. Aloya bunted him to second and Ed Rosch walked. Oscar Johnson beat out a hit to the right side, loading the bases. Simon North, trying for the squeeze, popped out. Then Joe Whittier hit the third pitch over the fence in left field for a grand-slam homer.

Simon North was throwing only fast balls. He was tremendously fast. One of the Auburn batters, swinging late, doubled down the left-field line in the third inning and another, swinging the same way, whistled a single over Whittier's head in the fourth. They made no time on the bases. After four full innings of play, Conway led 4 to 0 and North had struck out nine men.

"Pitch to ol' *George,* boy!" Crimeau yelled out as the fifth inning began, and North struck out the side. The Bears got another run in their half, and in the top half of the sixth inning Auburn got two walks and a single for its first run.

The visitors picked up another run in the seventh with another single, an error, and another pair of walks, but meanwhile North was striking men out. He had a total of sixteen through the seventh inning. He got two more in the eighth.

Then in the ninth inning he struck out the side. A great shout went up from the stands as the third man went down swinging. The noise from the crowd gained in intensity as the ball got through George Crimeau and skittered to the screen in front of the stands. The hitter, frozen momentarily in the classic, almost Grecian pose of completed, Ruthian swing, unwound and took off for first base. He beat the throw.

Stat Hunter called for time and came in to the mound. He beckoned to Crimeau and ol' George came out from behind the plate.

"George," the manager said. "Do that one more time and you're fined a hundred."

The catcher looked hurt. "Aw, *Stat,*" he said.

"Don't aw, Stat me," Hunter said.

"But I was thinkin' of th' *boy.*"

"Don't worry about the boy." Hunter slapped Simon North on the seat of his pants. "Let's go."

North struck out the next man, too, running his total for the game to twenty-two. This time Crimeau held the ball.

In the clubhouse, there was a telegram waiting for Stat Hunter. For one wild moment, the manager wondered how he could have received an answer from Marian so soon. Then he opened the envelope and saw that the telegram was from Ollie Marcus in Philadelphia.

It was a long telegram, and when he had finished reading it Hunter folded it up and put it in his coat pocket in his locker and walked over to Whittier. "I've got to have a talk with you."

"Now?"

"Soon as you get dressed."

"Jo Ann's waiting for me outside."

"She can hear this too."

"Where do you want to go?"

"Let's just sit in the car and talk outside."

Whittier shrugged his acquiescence.

When they got outside, Hunter and Whittier sat in the front seat and the girl, Jo Ann, sat in back, smoking a cigarette.

"I'll give it to you as fast as I know how," Hunter said to Whittier. "You remember the Cahill trade last winter, where there were three clubs mixed up in it. All right. Part of Philadelphia's end of the deal was to promise Boston a minor-league player to be named later. Now Boston wants you and may throw in a lefthander from a Class B club, and Philadelphia's interested because they'd like to give me a lefthander. Besides, Philadelphia doesn't like what it hears about you off the field."

"I quit all that," Whittier said.

"Okay," Hunter said. "Let's say you made a mistake and I made a mistake too. Even after I found out what you were doing with your money I didn't say anything about it right away because it didn't really occur to me that I should do anything about it so long as you were going the way you were on the field. But setting that to one side, what it comes down to is Philadelphia wants to leave it up to me and I'm going to leave it up to you. If you go now, you won't go straight up to the majors. Boston doesn't need help at second base, and it's a situation that probably would be good for you, because you'd get some regular work in the fast minors. If you stay here, then I'd say there was a good chance Philadelphia would call you up, at least after a while, and then you'd probably go up all the way. That's not saying you'd play regular or even stick in the big league, but that's the way it would probably fall."

Whittier said, "The big Bears are lousing up the joint, aren't they?"

"They're playing bad ball," Hunter said, "and the situation up there might change overnight. But you can't tell."

"Philadelphia knows about me and the money."

"That's right," Hunter said.

"Does Boston?"

"I don't know. I don't see any real good reason why they should."

"You don't like me, do you?"

"No," Hunter said. "I don't."

"The minute I make the jump out of here, even if just to a higher minor league, my salary goes up. That right?"

"That's right."

Sitting behind the wheel, Joe Whittier turned his head and said to the girl in back, "What do you think?"

"You do what you want," she said. "I don't care."

Hunter looked at her and saw she was looking at him in return, and he thought, *If Whittier takes the Boston thing, then she's alone and she wants me and she knows all about me and what's going to come of it? What's going to happen if she comes to my room again the way she did the other night and I haven't heard from Marian again in the meantime?*

You know what you'll do, he said to himself, and he thought, *Something straightens out and there's always something else. It's like those marching Chinese that Ripley used to have. What the hell good is it?*

Joe Whittier said now, "How long have I got?"

"I don't know," Hunter said. He glanced back at the girl again and then he opened his door and got out. "Sleep on it. Good night. Good night, Jo Ann."

"Good night, Stat," the girl said.

Andrew Hunter drove home and went to bed, after first placing the box with the clay ash tray very carefully on the shelf in the closet. The next day was a Saturday and Conway was going to open a four-game set with Waterloo, which was in first place now. Lying in his bed, Hunter decided to plan the series, but then he figured that it all depended on Whittier. If Whittier decided to go, maybe the new lefthander would arrive in time to be used against Waterloo, but then you had to find somebody to take Whittier's place at second base.

In his dreams, Hunter told himself that everything would be all right because a telegram had come from Marian saying she was coming back to him and bringing Janet with her, and it was the kind of dream you woke up from and, resuming sleep again, took up once more where you had left off. In the morning he knew there had been no telegram from Marian, and after he had had breakfast he went downtown to the Western Union main office, but they had nothing for him. He was not sure why he should expect a telegram from her, except that he knew he needed something from her, some word, and needed it urgently.

He picked up a morning paper, and there was a sports-page story about the decline and fall of the Philadelphia Bears. He hung around downtown for a while, and then he remembered that the dry goods store where Jo Ann worked as a salesgirl closed at noon on Saturdays, and he went over there and waited for her till she came out. She looked hot and a little tired, but at the same time she seemed glad to see him.

"Lunch?" he said.

"All right," she said. "You want to find out about last night."

He took her across the street to a restaurant that looked fairly clean, and they sat in a booth and had a cocktail. Jo Ann said, "I told him to take the Boston thing."

"What did he say?"

"He said he'd make up his mind today and let you know tonight."

"Why did you tell him to do that?"

"Because it was what I wanted to do." She looked away from him. "I don't care what you do about it. I'm not going to run at you any more. I wanted him gone and I wanted you here, and I think I understand about you."

"Sure you do." He said it gently.

"Don't tell me sure I do. You don't know whether I do or not. I think if you'd had a woman or even a lot of women after the—after she left you, then it wouldn't be hard and it wouldn't be a problem for you. But you didn't, and that made it tougher for you every day that came along, because you started thinking up reasons why you weren't sleeping with women, and after a while a reason got to be a reason just because you said it was a reason, whether it made any sense or not."

Hunter said, "There's more to it than just sleeping with somebody."

"I know it," she said, "but you're not giving yourself a chance to find out."

He saw that she had begun to cry, and he reached over and took her hands in his.

"It's all right," he said. "It's all right."

She shook her head. "I don't care if it's all right or not."

"Come on," he said, "the waiter's coming. Let's get something to eat. If Joe decides to go, then we'll see."

"Not you," she said. "You won't see about anything."

"I might," Stat Hunter said, and again he found himself hoping, almost frantically, that Marian would answer his telegram—answer it before it became too late. Now, though, he wondered too about what Jo Ann had said to him, about thinking up reasons just for the sake of having reasons, and he wondered how true it was.

There was no answer from Marian at all that day, and no valid reason under the sun why there should have been, and now Stat Hunter found himself hoping that Whittier would decide to stay in Conway. In the past, Andrew Hunter had been a man who did not like to make decisions. He had cured much of that these few months as manager of the Bears, but the difference now was that he had the fortitude—the foresight, perhaps—to make the right decision when it had to be made, rather than put it off.

Still, he told himself, he could not make a decision when he did not know if it was right or not; at least he did not want to, and the presence of Whittier in Conway would be an alibi for him with Jo Ann; would help him where he might not help himself.

But looking at Whittier before the night game with Waterloo, he sensed that the second baseman had decided to take the Boston offer. That way, for one thing, he probably could deadbeat the money he owed in Conway.

Whittier said nothing to the manager before the game, and during the game it became something not even thought about, because both pitchers were wild and Waterloo and Conway stood even at 4-4 after five innings, and there was a ball game to be won.

In the seventh inning, Harry Masick hit a single and came around on hits by Whittier and Hunter, and Conway led 5 to 4, and then in the top of the ninth, with two out and a man on first, the Waterloo batter lined one to left field.

Ed Rosch came in very fast for it, went into a belly dive, and came up holding the ball high. The base umpire, running into short left, started signaling downward with his palms, and in center field Stat Hunter saw that the umpire was calling it a hit, signaling that Rosch had trapped the ball, not caught it.

Rosch advanced toward the umpire yelling, and it did seem to Hunter that his man had made the catch. But he could not be sure with the tricks the lighting played in Fairchild Park, and meanwhile he saw the two Waterloo runners streaking around the bases.

"Throw the ball, Ed!" Hunter shouted. "Throw the ball!"

Still Rosch stood, talking and gesticulating in front of the umpire. Finally, as if coming out of a dream, he took the ball and sent it winging toward home plate. It was wild to the left and both runners were in, putting Waterloo ahead 6 to 5. Hands on his hips, Hunter waved to Vincent and North to get up in the bullpen. The angry Masick walked two men, and when he went to ball one on the next one, Hunter called for time and sent North in.

Simon got them out of the inning, and in the last of the ninth Rosch himself tied the score by singling Crimeau home from second. Ol' George made it with an immense, dusty slide.

They went to the eleventh, and then Hunter got a lead-off single and moved to third when Maraczewski hit safely to right field.

Hunter signaled Aloya to hit away, for the squeeze was too obvious and Aloya was not that good at bunting. Aloya flied to fairly shallow center field.

On third base, Stat Hunter waited, poised to start, watching Bo Walsh coaching at third. Walsh's arm was raised; when the center fielder made the catch, he would bring it downward, and Hunter would break with the signal rather than with the shouted word, because sight traveled faster than sound, even at so close a range.

Then Walsh's arm was down and Hunter was sprinting for the plate. He watched the catcher's feet, saw him lean forward and a little to the left, and went into a fallaway to the right. The catcher got the ball, but by this time Hunter's left foot, the leg bent acutely at the knee, was past him, and he dove instead for the man's body. The man's body swung away from him suddenly like a chair going around the corner in The Whip at an amusement park, and there was nothing there to tag. Stat Hunter was across with the winning run.

In the clubhouse, Hunter went straight to Ed Rosch. "Did you catch that ball?"

"No, Stat."

"Then why'd you argue? Why didn't you throw it in?"

"It would've tipped my hand."

Hunter found he was laughing. "Don't," he said, and laughed some more, "do that again."

"All right, Stat." Rosch was tremendously serious. "I won't."

Monk Gladstone said, "He only did it so Simon could get credit for another win," but he was smiling when he said it.

"Stat." It was old Jack Merced. "Telegram for you."

Andrew Hunter's thoughts left the ball game. This was it now. Marian. He sat down at his locker and opened it, and the first thing that came to his mind was disappointment such as he had rarely known, for again the same signature, that of Ollie Marcus of the Philadelphia Bears, stared up at him.

Then he read the telegram. He read it twice. He looked up then, and said in a loud voice, "All right. Now hear this. One of you's going up to Philadelphia."

There was a silence in the dressing-room, and the players looked at one another. This was something that rarely if ever happened to a Class C club—certainly not during the season.

Even assuming that Philadelphia was a loused-up club this year. Even assuming that somebody on the Conway club could help the big Bears.

Then, after a long moment, Simon North walked over to Joe Whittier and held out his hand. "Congratulations," he said.

But Whittier looked at Hunter, and Hunter shook his head slowly, wondering now how he should phrase it, how he ought to tell them. He had meant to save the second part of the telegram for later, but now he merely held the message out, and Monk Gladstone took it and read it and whistled, and then passed it on, and they all read it:

HAVE PITCHER NORTH REPORT TO PHILADELPHIA IMMEDIATELY. ALSO CALLING YOU UP TO MANAGE PHILADELPHIA AND WILL EXPECT YOU BY TUESDAY. REGARDS.

MARCUS

He told Jo Ann about it, the next day, over the telephone.

The first thing she said was, "You're not going, are you?"

"Don't be ridiculous."

"I'm not. I love you more than she ever loved you. What do you think of that?"

"What's that got to do with anything?"

"You're running away," Jo Ann said. Her voice was surprisingly even. "You're running away from me and you're running away from Walt Corio."

"*Corio?*"

"And don't forget," she said, "that Corio and I are friends. You're not going to do this because I'm not going to let you. If you think you've heard the last of me, you've got another think coming. I'm in love with you. Just remember that."

He knew then that she was a little crazy, but only a little, and in its way it frightened him.

CHAPTER FIVE
TWO AND TWO

WHITTIER TOOK THE BOSTON OFFER, and Monk Gladstone got the Conway Bears as manager. They gave Gladstone a lefthanded pitcher from Class A, Boston did, and Philadelphia scouted him up a second baseman from American Legion ball who was so bad Gladstone went with Bill O'Brien, his utility man, instead.

When he got to Philadelphia, Stat Hunter found Ollie Marcus waiting for him in the office of the Bears.

They shook hands and Hunter said, "What happened?"

Marcus shrugged his shoulders. "Something finally happened in this town that they couldn't blame on a busted water main. It's not going to be easy for you, Stat. This team is in bad shape."

"First things first," Hunter said. "Why me?"

Marcus put a toothpick in his mouth and stared amiably at the man sitting across the desk from him. Then he said "Morrison," and made a face. Morrison was the name of the deposed manager of the Philadelphia Bears. "Hell, Stat, why do you think we put you in Conway in the first place? Why do you think I came to town? What do you think those nightly reports we had you fill out were for? Do you think we have to scout our own players? Hell, that's what we had you there for. Sure, I got a look at the club when I came to town, but it was you I was looking at. I wanted to watch you handling a club. I wanted to watch you with your ballplayers. I saw the lead-off man get on base for you in an early inning and I saw you put the bunt on right away. You were playing for one run because you knew your pitcher only needed one run. That was big-league baseball, Stat. When you got more runs and you saw your pitcher was going for a no-hit game, you quit fooling around at bat so he could do his pitching while he was hot. That was big league all over again. When you got into a real bad jackpot with that gambling business, you handled it wonderfully, and when your team went sour you pulled them out."

"I didn't pull them out."

"The hell you didn't," Marcus said quietly. "The game you won with all those runs in the late innings ..."

"I wasn't even on the field then, when they won that one."

"That's just it. The umpire kicked you out. You beefed. You waited till you had a legitimate beef and then you let him have it till he threw you out. Earlier in the same game you pulled the old Henrich trap play, a play none of those Class C jokers ever saw before. When you walked off that field you left behind a ball club that had to win for you, Stat. I heard about that game and I said to T.H.—" T.H. was T. H. Hawes, president of the Philadelphia Bears "—I said, 'Stat Hunter's busted that slump for them and busted it for good. Watch them go now!' "

Marcus shifted the toothpick between his lips. Then he took it out of his mouth and used it between his fingers, for emphasis. "Stat, when we paid off Morrison and let him go it was because we had to. But we wouldn't have done it if we hadn't had a man to put in his place. You're it, old son. You've got this club and you can do any damn thing with it you want. What is it now? Coming on August. You've got two months, a little more, to put this club where it belongs. You put them in fourth place and you've got the club next season."

Marcus leaned back with his feet up on the desk. "People wonder how much a manager means to a club. Different people think different things about managers. They say a good manager can't help a club but a bad one can hurt it. No, sir." The scout shook his head profoundly. "A manager may be no better than his material, but he can be. It depends on what he does with that material. Give him the material going in. Then see what he does with it. Look at Durocher." Marcus put the toothpick back in his mouth. "Hell, what can I tell you? What is all this? Opinion. My opinion. Nothing more."

"Well," Hunter said, "I don't know."

"Nobody knows," Marcus said, "and that's a fact. How's Janet? What do you hear from Marian?"

"Nothing," Hunter said. "I guess they're all right."

"You think you've had troubles," the other man said, "wait till you see this club out here."

"Bad? Really bad?"

"When a winning ball club does nothing but lose," Marcus said, "this is not good. Oh, and one more thing. You can do what you want with yourself. You're still a playing manager."

"Avery's a good center fielder."

"You're a better one, if your arm can do it. Put Avery in right field. See? The front office is already telling you how to run your ball club."

"That's one thing," Stat Hunter said, "that we had no trouble with at Conway."

"On the other hand," Marcus said, "you wound up at Conway without a lefthander. That certainly won't happen to you with these Bears. You got five lefthanders." The toothpick shifted. "Each one's worse than the next."

"Another thing," Hunter said. "At least in this league you've got a league president that doesn't give you the willies. Some time I'll tell you about Ironton Farney Kane."

"I know all about Ironton Farney Kane. You still didn't know when you were well off."

"Well," Hunter said, "you called me up here. I didn't ask to come."

"No," Marcus said, "but you were relieved. I could tell by looking at you. If I know you, you probably had a broad taking a run at you, and with all this latter-day nobility of yours you weren't quite sure what you were going to do. So I saved your bacon."

Hunter looked away. He thought of Jo Ann and wondered whether he had been saved or not. Out loud, he said, "You should have been an insurance adjuster."

"I was," Marcus said, "for seven years."

If you asked someone like Stat Hunter what the difference was between classifications in baseball, he would probably say that, to begin with, you expected them to make the plays in the majors that you could only hope they might make in the minors.

It was more complex than that. You became more sure of yourself as you stepped upward through the minors, but by the time you were in the fast minors it became hard to discern, because baseball was a game simultaneously of offense and defense, and for every hit behind the runner you might expect to find a fielder looking for the play. By the time you drew the line between triple-A ball and the big leagues, you would be down to one thing—pitching—and even then, it was little more than a generality.

Even now, it was not the same in the big league as it had been in Stat Hunter's time, before the war. He could remember when the National League alone had at least five shortstops who at their peaks were better than just about anyone in that league today—Jurges with Chicago, Durocher with St. Louis, Vaughan with Pittsburgh, Bartell with New York, Eddie Miller with Boston. There were catchers like Hartnett, Lombardi, Banning, and Lopez.

The very late 1930's—'36, '37, '38, '39, and '40—those were the baseball years Stat Hunter remembered the best. What the years before that were like, he did not recall so definitely, but he did remember the seasons before the war: Elbie Fletcher, the best fielding first baseman he ever saw, and big Mize coming up with St. Louis, and McCormick at Cincinnati, slick in the field for a big man, for a righthander who played first, and Dolph Camilli and Buddy Hassett and Gus Suhr. There were Herman and Whitehead and Cuccinello and Linus Frey, and third basemen like Werber and Hack and Lavagetto. When the New York Giants needed pitchers to start ball games, they would call on Hubbell or Melton or Fitzsimmons or Schumacher or Harry Gumbert— and what club in the majors today would or could rotate five men like that at you?

There were outfielders like the Waners and Terry Moore and Ott, and you could do the same with the other league, starting with the Yankees in an era where their Newark farm club in the International League was so good in itself that today it would be a first-division team in the majors.

There was no Luke Appling in the majors now, and Joe Kuhel was gone. In those days you had second basemen named Gordon and Doerr—and look at second base in the American League today. Pitchers: Feller, Grove, Gomez, Ruffing. You could do it team by team, if you wanted to.

It was something Andrew Hunter went over in his mind every now and again. He could build up a convincing case, but even so he was not always certain how much of it was records and performances and statistics, how much of it simply that those were less complicated days, and undoubtedly happier. Baseball today? It had Musial, Robinson, Campanella, Spahn, Kiner, Rosen, Lemon, Kell, Williams, Rizzuto, Mantle, Zernial, Pierce, Carrasquel, Snider, Reese, Vernon, Furillo, Roberts, Simmons, Fain, Mathews, Berra—and you could go on. It had its ballplayer's ballplayers, top men, like Eddie Yost at Washington, and it had the most exciting center fielder Stat Hunter had ever watched: Willie Mays.

Hunter was on the sidewalk outside the Bears' downtown office building now; it was not yet noon, and he flagged a cab and told the driver he wanted the ball park.

The driver said, without turning his head, "What for?"

"That's a good question," Stat Hunter said. "Sometimes I wonder that myself."

"You and me both," the driver said. "You want to go out Broad Street?"

"All right," Hunter said.

"Elsewhere they're collecting garbage," the driver said. "It's not often I get a fare for the ball park. I mean when they're playing and when they ain't playing. You got to be a little crazy to go out and see the Bears, that's my thought. Then I get a guy like you who just wants to go the ball park when they're not playing. You know something, mister, I think you may be smarter than all the rest of us put together. The Bears ain't playing, so the man says take me to the ball park." The driver tapped his temple. "This is dumb? No, says I. This man you got in the back seat of your hack may be the smartest man in Philadelphia. Goes out to the ball park, buys himself a box seat, maybe, and he still don't have to watch the Bears. I am just beginning to think to myself how smart this is."

Hunter said, "I see you don't fancy the Bears."

"I fancy the Bears in Saskatchewan," the driver said. "They got a club, it's a good club. They got pitchers as good as anything in the league. They got speed, they got a couple of boys hit that long ball pretty good. They're pretty good baserunners. That shortstop they got is a slick glove man—a real slick glove man. They got some experience, they got some youth. In short, mister, they got everything. This is why they're in sixth place."

"What do you think is wrong?"

"I don't know," the driver said. "They got this man Hunter coming in to take over and I figure he's got it made, because if he don't do nothing but sit in the dugout and cut out paper dolls he's got that Morrison beat five ways. Many's the time I watched Stat Hunter play when he was in the big league."

"What'd you think of him?"

"All right," the driver said. "All right. If his legs hadn't got tired he'd be up there yet."

"I heard it was his arm."

The driver shook his head. "His legs, mister."

They drove in silence for a time. Then Hunter said, "Think Hunter'll do much playing for them?"

The cab driver made an expressive sound. "What does he want to play for? He's an old man."

"He's only thirty-seven."

"This is young?" the driver wanted to know. "You want to open a vegetable stand, go out with a pushcart and an umbrella, all right. So you're thirty-seven years old. Go ahead. Who's stopping you? Baseball—what, are you crazy? What can I tell you, mister? Fifteen years I been pushing a hack. My brother says to me, open a store. Sure, open a store. Make money, they take it from you in taxes. Lose money, you go out of business. Break even, the CIO puts a picket in front of the door. What the hell good is it? Let him sit on the bench where he belongs."

Hunter was laughing in the back seat. "You're a funny guy."

"Sure, I'm a funny guy. People drop dead laughing at me in the back seat, I can't collect a fare. Drive with your mouth shut, you go stir crazy. Open your mouth, you're a Communist."

"You're quite a philosopher."

"I can still break an axle on Lehigh Avenue. Who's going to tow me in?"

"The tow truck," Hunter said, laughing. "How'd we get on this? We started out talking about the Philadelphia Bears."

"What about them?"

"I don't know. What about them?"

"Screw the Philadelphia Bears," the cab driver said.

These were the Philadelphia Bears: Connover and Peterkin catching, Dog-face Martin at first base, Kramer and Laws alternating at second base, Bob McNeil at short, Lynn Watson at third base. Smith, Avery and Goodman in the outfield, with Larsen and Potts for extra outfield. Hines and Jaretski and Lindeman and Sampson, the frontline righthanders, and Geller and Matson and Hobo Bates, the best lefthanders. That was the squad that mattered; the others were the best that could be had, none of them top-liners.

Morrison, the manager they booted, had played a different line-up every day, or so it seemed, and it had not done much good. Even in sixth place, the Bears were around .450 in the standings, which meant two things: they could beat any other club in the league, as they had; and the seventh- and eighth-place teams were very bad, as they were.

St. Louis had been a surprise this year, had been in the first division all season long, so one excuse for Philadelphia could be St. Louis, but it was a stinking excuse. Morrison had used his pitchers badly: this much Hunter knew. Hines had been hot at the start of the season, and Morrison had gone to get out in front of the race, and he was working Hines every fourth game with a relief call or two thrown in. Hines lost two four-hitters in a row and the next time he started Chicago belted him out of there, and New York did the same thing the time after that. Morrison had thought Jesse Goodman was the kind of outfielder who needed to be rested against lefthanders, and he had used Larsen in there instead when a lefthander went against them. The Bears saw a lot of lefthanders. Larsen did not know how to play the wall, and he hurt them, hurt them more than he made up for with his bat. In one game, with one out in the ninth and a Chicago runner on third base and the score tied, he had caught a long foul fly instead of letting it drop, and the runner had come home on the catch to win the game.

Morrison had not believed in giving his pitchers the call in advance. Once between games of a double header against New York, Milt Sampson was washing a double salami sandwich down with a Pepsi-Cola and Morrison said to him, "Milt, you're working the second game."

"For Christ sake," Sampson had said. "Are you nuts?"

"If you want to chicken out, just say so," Morrison said, and when Sampson got into a hole in the fifth inning he left him in there while New York scored eight runs.

"No son of a bitch is going to tell me how to run my club," Morrison told the reporters afterward. "If he learns to pitch his way out of jams, maybe some day he'll be a pitcher."

All this, Stat Hunter had found out in advance, but it was not simply the fact that Morrison was not liked by his players. To begin with, Morrison had had some favorites on the club: Bob McNeil, the rookie shortstop who won all the raves with his fielding, was one. Morrison had been a shortstop during his playing days, and it was profitable for him to build up McNeil, because the papers thus would credit Morrison automatically for—as one sports page put it—"spending endless painstaking hours and bringing the youngster along." Jack Connover, the catcher, had come to Philadelphia in an early-season trade for another catcher who had refused to take any lip from Morrison. This stamped Connover as a Morrison man, and Connover went along, because Morrison treated him handsomely, knowing what it would look like if a second catcher were to oppose him after he had got rid of the first.

There were others that Morrison had liked, too, but it was not even so clear-cut as having the club split into two camps. Two of the coaches on the Bears, Dave Donald and Mike Schwartz, had been angling quietly for Morrison's job ever since it became apparent the manager would be deposed. Gently and politically, they had lined up their own supporters.

Added to this, there was the handful of players that owed allegiance to no man, for various reasons—like Dogface Martin, the hard-hitting first baseman, who got along with everybody, and Jim Potts, the reserve outfielder, who simply did not give a damn.

Even then, you could not say all right, they are lined up in four separate camps, because some of the players' devotions overlapped, and some switched allegiance overnight, and there was the added fact of the obvious line of demarcation between those who played regularly and those who did not, and the natural inclinations of the old-timers on the team to stick together to the exclusion of the newcomers, and—above everything else—the unhappy reality of the players' disliking and distrusting one another.

Kramer at second base had messed up a ground ball to put Tom Jaretski, the pitcher, into a hole he could not escape only four days ago, and the two players had tangled afterward under the stands. Goodman was not talking to Geller and Hobo Bates was not talking to anybody.

They had only one thing in common, these disenchanted professionals: they resented Stat Hunter.

At Conway, Hunter was clearly the leader, the only man on the squad who had played in the majors, and most of his players were very young men. On this team they were all big leaguers and Hunter was a man coming from the minors to take a job one of them or one of their friends might have had and to tell them what to do. Managing a sixth-place club might not be heaven, but it was a manager's job in the big league, and that was enough said.

The only one who did not resent Hunter was Moses Jones, the relief pitcher, and he did not count, because he was the only colored player on the squad. Moses was younger than Satchel Paige, to whom he had often been compared, but not much younger. He differed from Paige in build, being on the short and dumpy side, but his arm was equally rubbery and his outlook equally mournful. Heat was the only thing he liked. He would cut his pitching sleeve to the shoulder on hot days in the bullpen, to bake the arm, and mornings and off-days he liked nothing better than to show up at the ball park and lie down under the heat lamp.

He and Hunter had run across each other in barnstorming games time and again over the years, and each had a healthy respect for the other. The Bears had called Moses Jones out of the obscurity of a touring, clowning team which at the time was in Salem, Oregon, in a patent effort to bolster the gate by bringing in colored fans, but Moses had saved games for them, too, and his presence on the team called for an immediate exercise of sports-writing ingenuity in a drive to dress him with a suitable nickname. It had to be a nickname equal to The Splendid Splinter, The Sultan of Swat, The Meal Ticket, The Gay Señor, The Big Train, The Yankee Clipper, and The Peerless Leader—and, as finally formulated by a columnist for an afternoon paper, it was. So now they all called him Ol' Man Mose.

Mose was lying on the rubbing table with his eyes closed, alone in the room, when Stat Hunter came into the Philadelphia clubhouse. The first thing Hunter thought of was Ironton Farney Kane.

Then he said, "Hello, Mose. How you feel?"

Moses Jones opened his eyes, slowly and reluctantly. "Well, it's Stat," he said thoughtfully. "Hey, Stat."

"I'm early," Hunter said. "I called a clubhouse meeting for two o'clock."

"Might as well be early," the pitcher said, and lay back and closed his eyes once again. "Might as well enjoy it while it's peaceful."

"Doesn't figure to be peaceful?"

"Figures to be anything but." The pitcher sat up on the table. "Stat, I heard a little about you up in that bush league where you was managing. Utica, where you was. I got to tell you something. You never seen nothing of trouble till you been here. You don't got to be here long. You don't got to be here a week, even. Be here one night is all. Tonight they got to play New York in a night game. That's all."

"It can't be that bad."

Moses Jones rubbed his pitching shoulder reflectively. "No? Stat, we've done screwed up thirty ball games. I don't mean lost 'em, we've screwed 'em up ourselves. That Morrison. He tells me I can't go nine innings. So what do he do? He bring me in in the fourth inning and I pitch to the fifteenth. But I can't go nine innings. I can't start for him. He bring me in in the fourth inning, we can't be better than a run ahead, prob'ly we tied, maybe we even behind already. What I got to do, I got to come in with men on bases and the big men coming up and I got to come in throwing strikes. Morrison says to me don't throw nothing good but don't walk nobody. He want me to *eat* the ball."

"Well," Hunter said, "like a cab driver said to me coming out to the ball park, I can't do worse than Morrison."

"You ain't seen this club," Moses Jones said, and eased himself back down on the table.

Hunter held two clubhouse meetings that day—one in the afternoon, where he shook hands with everyone and went over the signs; the other just before they went out for pre-game practice before the night game with New York.

The manager had not liked what he had seen that afternoon, had not liked what he had felt. Thus he had deliberately held off on his pitching nominations until tonight. Now he faced his players, and he said:

"Batting order tonight McNeil, Avery, Goodman, Martin, Smith, Watson, Connover, Kramer."

Kyle Smith, the right fielder said, "Who's pitching, Stat?"

"Him," Stat Hunter said, and pointed directly at Simon North, the young righthander who had arrived from Conway three days before.

The players were looking at one another. What they had known of Andrew Hunter was not this. Hunter was the kind of man who would go along with the status quo, would feel his way, would try to bring men together. Hunter, the Hunter some of them had known in the big leagues in years gone by, never shocked anyone. Maybe something had happened to him in that bush-league town.

While they were looking at one another, Stat Hunter moved easily to the little room off the clubhouse that served as the manager's office. He was not quite through with them yet. When he got to the door of his office, he turned to face them again.

"And Moses Jones starts tomorrow," he said, and went into the little office, closing the door behind him.

New York was leading the league—four full games ahead of second-place Chicago—and they were throwing their best lefthander against the Bears tonight. He was three-and-one against the Bears on the season. As a vote of confidence in his men, Hunter had started Goodman in left field tonight, something Morrison would never have done against a lefthander, but now, sitting in the dugout with the noise of the crowd spinning in his ears, Hunter found himself wondering if Goodman would ever come to bat. Simon North had walked the first two men and the third one had singled to right field for a run, sending the tail runner to third.

If you thought a minor league crowd could let you have it, then it was only because you had forgotten what a major league crowd could do. There were more than 25,000 in the Bears' park tonight, drawn by the twin fascinations of New York and a new Philadelphia manager—not to mention the fact that pre-season sales, before anybody knew the Bears would be out of it, had been brisk, and tonight's game had seemed a natural in advance.

The Bears were out of it. Stat Hunter entertained no pennant notions. They trailed the leaders by twenty-one games. But even more important, they were in sixth place. It was an axiom in baseball that it was better to be in second place ten games out than in fourth place five games out. If you were in second place, then it was up to you. Thus had the Giants of 1951 caught the Dodgers from thirteen and a half games back in mid-August even though the Dodgers played better than .500 ball all the way from there to the end.

But even if you were no farther back than fourth, and you got hot, then still everything was against you. You had no assurance that three clubs in front of you, or any one of them, would fail to get hot too, which made it just three times as tough as when you were in second place. Furthermore, they would be playing each other, and someone would have to win.

Get up to fourth place, Marcus had told him, and Stat Hunter knew how tough that would be. He had not reckoned with its being tough in the top half of the first inning of the first game he managed, but here was his shock therapy working mightily in reverse, and the stands were on him unmercifully.

Now North went to two-and-nothing on the New York clean-up man, and Hunter waved his right hand to the bullpen and called for time and walked out to the mound. In the bullpen, Moses Jones came slowly to his feet and started to work.

Jack Connover, the catcher, came out, and Steve Kramer came over from second base. Hunter was chewing three sticks of spearmint gum, chewing rapidly. He said to Connover, "What about it?"

"I don't know," Connover said. "What about it?"

"Well," Hunter said, "what do you think?"

"What do you think, Steve?" Connover said.

"I don't know what I think," Steve Kramer said.

It dawned on Stat Hunter that they had decided to go along with the new manager, first because he had surprised them in the clubhouse before the game, second because there was no percentage in acting otherwise. Whatever happened now would be Hunter's fault. They knew it, so they were giving him rope.

Still, Hunter appreciated it. What they were doing now was talking in circles so that Moses Jones, out in the bullpen, could get the maximum time in which to heat up. Now, out in left field, Jesse Goodman waved for the club trainer. The trainer went trotting out there, and the plate umpire came out and said, "You bring all this up from Class C, Stat?"

"Not all of it," Hunter said.

"What's the matter with your left fielder?"

"Due to an accident at birth," Stat Hunter said, "I was born without the ability to read minds. I don't know."

The plate umpire turned and said to the third-base umpire, "Get out and see what that is."

The third-base umpire went dutifully trotting out to left field. The plate umpire returned to his position, and Hunter said to Connover, "He's fast, isn't he?"

"Damn fast."

"Strong?"

"Sure he's strong. What do you mean?"

"And wild?"

"You saw me," Connover said. "I put my arm out of whack reaching for that curve ball."

"All right," Stat Hunter said. "Call the fast ball. Now get out of here. I want to tell him something private."

Connover and Kramer went away and Stat Hunter looked at Simon North. He said, "Simon, this is going to be a speech. It's going to be a speech because you're scared. You're so scared you can't move."

Simon North nodded without speaking. His Adam's apple moved up and down.

"All right," Hunter said. "Now you're going to hear something from me you never heard before. You're going to be pitching nothing but fast balls, and it's going to be like you're pitching batting practice. I want you to lay it in there. I'm going to show you something. You've got major leaguers behind you. I'm going to show you how they can go and get the ball when it's hit. You're going to see things you never dreamed of. You've got my guarantee. That's number one. Number two is this. You've got the best relief pitcher in baseball. This isn't Conway, Simon. This isn't deciding you've got to strike out everybody you pitch against because if you don't there's nobody to make the play behind you. This is the big league, Simon. There are pitchers in this league who've made a career of just letting batters hit the ball and then having their fielders go get it. If I didn't think you could do that, I wouldn't have let them call you up here. All right?"

Simon North nodded, slowly.

"Oh," Hunter said, "one more thing. A man can get in situations that affect his life, and for you this isn't one of them. You won't believe this. When I was thirteen years old back in Long Island City I bet my father fifty dollars I'd never get married, because I didn't see where it made any sense, and you probably don't see where it makes any sense when I tell you now that this isn't going to kill you one way or the other. I'm just saying it to you for whatever good it's going to do. Go ahead and pitch the ball. The hell with it."

He turned and walked with definite stride back toward the dugout. When he got there, he turned and saw the trainer coming down the steps behind him.

"What was wrong with that outfielder?"

"Nothing," the trainer said.

"What'd you tell the umpire?"

"Finger."

Hunter nodded. "What'd the umpire say?"

"He told me what was going to happen with the next finger."

"Well," Stat Hunter said, "you're built for it."

"Morrison was a funny guy too," the trainer said, and they both sat down, side by side, watching Simon North getting ready to pitch again.

Connover called for the fast ball, and North poured it over for a strike, and the sound of it hitting Connover's mitt brought an "oooh" from the stands. Still, it had been two-and-nothing, and the hitter was taking. He was expecting fast balls, too, and still he let the next one go by in a kind of awe. It was another strike.

He swung at the next one. He swung hard, and still he swung late. He hit nothing. He sat down on his pants in the batter's box.

The infield talked it up behind Simon North. He got two strikes on the next batter. Hunter prayed he would waste the next one, but he came across at the knees with it and the batter put it on the ground over the mound. Bob McNeil came over from shortstop, moving like a current of air, gloved it a stride to the left and back of second base, kicked the bag and threw to first for the double play.

When North got to the dugout, Stat Hunter said to him, "See what I mean?"

"I see."

"And don't throw them balls to hit at on nothing-and-two. You knew better than that at Conway."

"All right," Simon said, and sat down.

He was tremendously fast over the next four innings, and already he had claimed eight strike-out victims. But Philadelphia had moved only one man to second meanwhile. In the last of the fifth, Kramer drew a lead-off walk. Hunter wanted the tie for now. He had North bunt, but it went badly and they got the force at second base. McNeil got a line single to right field, and North held at second. Avery flied very deep to right, moving North to third on the catch, and then Goodman hit on the ground to the third baseman. Goodman was a fast man, and the throw to first was in the dirt. He beat it. Simon North, who had not moved until he saw the throw going to first, raced for the plate and was thrown out on the sequence, the first baseman to the catcher.

With the crowd buzzing over the exciting mechanics of the play that had just unfolded, North picked himself out of the dirt and headed out for the mound. He was already there before he realized he had forgotten his glove, and he had to go and get it, then return to the mound.

Mike Schwartz, who had been coaching at third base, came down the dugout steps with an elaborate shrug. "Don't you teach them how to run in the minors?"

Hunter said, "Maybe he'd forgotten there were two out."

"I told him there were two out."

"Well, he looked like he was afraid there was going to be a play on him."

"How crazy can you get?"

"Anyway," Hunter said, "in the minors he could hold up and still make it home. They don't have first basemen like that in Class C."

"New rule," Schwartz said. "When on third base with two out always hold up on a ground ball."

"Leave it alone," Hunter said. "You're right, Mike. You know you're right."

"Okay," Schwartz said. "Who said anything?"

North's fast ball was just as fast as it had been, but now he was gone again on his control. He walked the first man to face him, and Hunter waved for Moses Jones to get heated again. The next batter caught the second pitch and rode it on a soaring line into right-center field. Back at the fence, beneath one of the arc-light standards, Kyle Smith caught the ball running, going away.

The next man singled sharply to left, and when North went to ball one on the following hitter, Hunter called for time and went out to the mound. He said, "That's all tonight, Simon. Let's see the ball."

Simon North looked at him, and the manager saw that his young pitcher was close to tears. "You did some running last inning," Hunter said, "and we did some hitting. This inning we've got some big men coming up. If they start anything, I'd pinch-hit for you anyway. So we'll do it this way. You struck out a lot of men. We're proud of you."

North said, "What do I do now?"

"Wait for Mose to get here and then just walk to the dugout," Hunter said. "I'll walk with you."

Moses Jones moved slowly onto the scene. He said to Hunter, "Thought I was going to start tomorrow."

"You are."

Jones said nothing, but Hunter caught the shadow of a smile on his face. The relief pitcher started throwing to Connover, and Hunter slapped North on the seat of the pants, and the two of them started for the dugout.

Fans came to their feet to applaud the young pitcher as he left the field. Hunter knew what the thrill was like. Looking at Simon North, he could see the young pitcher felt it too.

Moses Jones threw four pitches and was out of the inning on a pair of infield flies. He would have made it on two pitches, save for the fact that neither hitter would touch the first ball.

Dog-face Martin led off the last half of the sixth inning with a giant home run over the right-field wall. The players grouped happily to meet him and grasp his hand as he returned to the dugout, something they had not done quite so professionally before television, and Hunter found himself thinking that if Simon North had come home without hesitating on that last play in the fifth, Philadelphia now would be in front 4 to 1 rather than tied 1 to 1. Some of the other members of the Bears, he sensed, were thinking the same thing.

That was all Philadelphia got in the sixth. New York worked Jones for a run in the seventh, a run fashioned in the main around Connover's overthrow of second base on a steal, but in the last of the eighth, with one out, Smith and Watson both singled, the former going to third base.

The play for Stat Hunter now was to replace his hitter, Jack Connover, with a faster man, to reduce the chance of a double play. He looked over his bench. Then he picked out two bats and came up the steps of the dugout.

The crowd began to roar. This was more than surprise—more even than recognition on the part of the fans that the new manager already had made his presence felt, in his first game.

This was the fans' welcome back to the big leagues for Andrew Hunter. Many times through the years they had seen him before. Now he was one of theirs, and they were not sorry. They stood up and cheered, and the announcer growled, "Number Thirty-seven, Stat Hunter, batting for Connover."

He thought, *If Marian could hear this....*

But instantly his thoughts were back with the game. What would happen if he got on? If they tied it? Kramer, Jones, McNeil, Avery, Goodman to follow him. Not a real long ball until Dog-face Martin, back of Goodman. If he pinch-hit a man for Moses Jones, then he had to come back with another pitcher in the ninth. Matson and Lindeman were working in the Bears' bullpen, but neither was a tight pitcher like Jones. On the other hand, if he bunted the run across to tie it now, then took his chances on Kramer and Jones behind him, he would have at least a tie going into the ninth and the top of his order ready to hit.

Hunter was thinking not only as Stat Hunter, the Philadelphia manager. He was trying to think also as the New York manager. Stepping up to bat now, he made up his mind to wait for one pitch—and see.

New York figured him for the take. The lefthander gunned a strike over the heart of the plate. As he did, Stat Hunter's hand moved imperceptibly along the bat.

Now the next pitch was ready, and still Hunter did not signal the squeeze. Out of the corner of his eye, he saw the bait had caught its fish. Gently crouched, the New York third baseman was on his toes, leaning a little too much toward the plate.

The pitch rode in and the third baseman was coming in with it. Stat Hunter's bat whipped around and the ball whistled toward third base, a foot fair, flashing past the trapped fielder and out along the left-field line.

Smith rode home from third base with the tying run. The New York left fielder was digging the ball out on its third low bounce off the fence, and as he straightened up, Lynn Watson was turning wide and rocketing over third base, getting the wave from Mike Schwartz down the line and heading for home. The shortstop's throw from the relay slot in left field was for the plate, aimed at cutting down the lead run, and Stat Hunter, coming around second base now, kept going.

They let the throw ride through and Watson beat it with a long slide. The catcher came out of the tag and shot the ball to third. Hunter went in on the outfield side of the bag and beat it. Noise from the stands was tremendous.

New York was going to pitch to Kramer. Hunter put on the bunt. It rolled toward the first baseman; he could not make up his mind about a play, and everybody was safe. Then Moses Jones struck out and Kramer was down stealing, but Philadelphia had the lead now, 4 to 2, and when the inning was over Hunter told himself *the hell with it,* and went out to center field to take Avery's place.

Moses Jones did no fooling in the top of the ninth. He got two men on ground balls. The next man, a pinch hitter, hit a tall one to center field. Stat Hunter waited under it, moved the gum around in his mouth, caught the ball, and they were loping toward the clubhouse now, the fans roaring their approval.

The Bears in the clubhouse were happy ballplayers, but they still were not relaxed. Tonight's had been a tense game, for one thing; they still were in sixth place, for another. Bill Avery came over to Stat Hunter and said, "Have I still got a job?"

"Hell, yes," Hunter said.

"Why?"

Hunter looked up from the bench in front of his locker. "Because if I make three long throws I can't throw another ball for a week. I'm good for an inning here and there. That's about all I'm good for."

"Just asking," Avery said, but he looked relieved

The morning papers the next day hailed Hunter to a fault. When he got to the ball park for the afternoon game against New York there was already a line at the unreserved windows. Stat Hunter grinned and went into the clubhouse, and what was waiting for him there was an air-mail letter from Nebraska.

He knew the handwriting. He went into the small room that was his office and opened it and read:

Dear Stat,

Your wire came and I'll have some pictures to send, very soon, I hope. Meanwhile I heard about your getting the Philadelphia job and you know I wish you all the good fortune in the world. I hope that now you have everything you want.

Janet made an ash tray for you and sent it to you. It was a little while before you left Conway. She's looking forward to seeing you in the fall. Do you want me to have her count on it? I know that your new job may keep you busy in the East even after the season is over.

As ever,
Marian

Hunter read it over three times. He read between the lines, and over them and under them, and tried to interpret and to interpolate; tried to think as Marian might be thinking, though of course he could not, and did not really want to.

He decided he would answer it at once—briefly but warmly, on the stationery of the Philadelphia Bears:

Dear Marian,

Thanks for your note. I hope you are well, as I am. The new job is a challenge, but I am not as devoted to baseball—maybe devoted is not a good word, but you will know what I mean. I love the game still, but it is not the same as before. Maybe there are reasons for that too.

I got the ash tray and am writing to Janet tonight. Tell her I will be there after the season as fast as my legs can carry me.

Love,

Stat

They had nearly fifteen thousand for the weekday game against New York, and today Hunter had the Bears running. McNeil and Avery worked the double steal in the bottom of the first, and Martin's single through the right side brought both of them in. New York got a run in the third and three more in the fifth, all three on a home run, but Hunter talked to Moses Jones and left him in. In the last of the sixth, Goodman, Martin, Smith, and Watson singled in order for two runs and Jack Connover flied deep for another. In the last of the seventh Avery singled and Goodman tripled, and Philadelphia had the game, 6 to 4. Moses Jones went all the way, and they got him for only six hits.

That was the way it began for Stat Hunter. By mid-August he had the club in fifth place; as August ended they had taken fourth away from St. Louis. Labor Day came and New York led the league by three games. Boston was in second place, seven games ahead of Chicago. Chicago was three games in front of Philadelphia.

Hunter had set his sights on third place, but it was going to be tough. They hit Chicago on the final western swing, and in four games the best they could do was break square. Simon North and Gerald Hines won for the Bears; Jaretski and Sampson lost.

St. Louis, meanwhile, took three out of four from Boston. This did not help Boston's pennant chances, but did them no tremendous harm, for New York also was stalled, unable to make the daylight stretch. It did mean, though, that St. Louis might be coming on again—ready, perhaps, to take fourth place back from the Bears.

They moved into St. Louis for a three-game set, all of them night games. Hunter was using Jaretski, Hines, Sampson, and Hobo Bates as his regular four pitchers, using North and Moses Jones for spot starting work, using Jones, Lindeman, Geller, and Matson in relief. He had Bates for the opener against St. Louis, and Hobo got pinned 10 to 4. Jaretski won the second for them when Lynn Watson homered in the eighth, 4 to 3.

That left one more game, a big one, and Hunter went with Hines, his top winner. Hines had won sixteen on the year so far, and had beaten St. Louis four times.

St. Louis got to him for a run in the first, on an inside-the-park home run, a long shot that Avery misjudged badly, then let carom away. Still, Stat Hunter figured that three runs would be all Hines would need to win. He tried to get them singly, but events went badly, and he saw two runners cut down at third base.

It was the top half of the fifth inning before Philadelphia scored. Martin and Smith doubled back-to-back off the high screen in right field, to tie it at 1-1. But in the home half, St. Louis had a walk, an error, and a ground single to left field to put together for another run, and they led it, 2 to 1.

They went that way to the seventh. Then Bob McNeil, leading off for the Bears, dropped a double among three converging St. Louis defenders in short left-center field. Having reached second base, he then stepped off the bag, and the St. Louis shortstop immediately tagged him with the ball.

McNeil came back to the bench, looking at his shoes as he came down the dugout steps. Hunter said, "What did he say to you?"

The young Philadelphia shortstop looked at his manager. "I'm sorry, Stat. I suckered."

"What'd he say?"

"He said to me, 'Bob, step off the bag for a minute so I can straighten it.' So I stepped off." McNeil went and sat by himself at the end of the bench. And try as they could, the Bears could not get another run for Hines. They lost the game 2 to 1 and now were ahead of St. Louis in the standings by just one game.

These last three weeks of the season would tell the story. Hunter's mind reeled with plans, with performances and statistics, when he got back to his hotel. Underneath his door, as he entered his room, he saw a house message. It was teletyped:

MR. HUNTER, RM 563,
1015P CALL OPR 14 OMAHA NEBRASKA

Hunter picked up the phone, and after the long and always exasperating channels you had to go through to trace back a long-distance call, he found himself talking to Marian's father, on the farm in their small town outside of Omaha.

"Stat? That you?"

"Yes," Hunter said. "It's me. What's up?"

"It's Janet," Marian's father said. "She's disappeared. We-"

"She's what?"

"Gone," the telephone said. The voice sounded very tired. "She isn't here. We—"

"I'll be there," Hunter said, and he hung up the phone. An ordinary father might perhaps have wanted to hear more information. The Stat Hunter of old, caught in the middle of a tough pennant race, would have wanted to hear much, much more.

But now Stat Hunter picked up the phone again and called the home of a St. Louis sports editor, an old friend.

He told him what had happened. "Do this for me," the manager said. "Get me on the next plane for Omaha and get me one of those rented cars at the Omaha airport. Then call Mike Schwartz at the hotel here and tell him he's got the team till I get back and I'll be in touch with him. I'm leaving for the airport right now. Get a message out there some way so I can find out what plane I'm on."

"Will do," the sports editor said, and hung up.

Andrew Hunter did not pack his bag. He got a cab to the St. Louis airport, and found that the next plane for Omaha would not leave until three o'clock in the morning. He sat at the lunch counter there, drinking black coffee and staring at an advertising display sign that had moving cardboard figures going around in a circle.

The plane ride was bumpy and dark, and he sat looking out the window at the redness of the engine cowlings. In the darkness of early morning at the Omaha airport, the automobile was waiting for him. He knew the way, and while he was driving he switched on the radio.

The headlights of the car made the emptiness of the two-lane state highway seem even more black; in the sky there were gray clouds that moved in darting gusts with the wind. The radio had an all-night record program, and now a girl was singing:

"Can I forget you?
Or will my heart remind me
That once we walked in a moonlit dream?"

There was no moon tonight. Andrew Hunter looked at the speedometer. It held, seeming not to move, just over the figure *70*. The chill of the night at pre-dawn moved in on the manager of the Philadelphia Bears, moving through the thin summer suit he wore so that he could feel it in his bones and muscles, and his right shoulder felt like it had made the throw from deepest center field at the Polo Grounds.

The clock on the dashboard said it was five o'clock, and behind him the sky was turning light, a slow, inexorable light that was first brown and then was a color at once deeper and less deep. The call letters of the radio station came through, and then a man's voice:

"What are you looking for, men? That new Buick or Cadillac? A suit of clothes so you can take out the girl friend in the snappy style to which she's accustomed? Money to pay off those old doctor's bills, emergencies, the rent, or payments on that new refrigerator or automatic dryer for that good friend of yours the wife? Now you can have that money, borrow it on those long-stretch eee-asy terms from Reliable Finance, eastern Nebraska's oldest and friendliest plan to provide that extra cash. Have you got a job, a car, insurance policies, or a home? You'll get that money you need in strict confidence, in strict privacy, at any of the fourteen offices of Reliable Finance.

"And now the five o'clock news. The daughter of baseball star Andrew Hunter, that's the manager of the Philadelphia Bears, has disappeared from her home in Stillwell, sixty-four miles northwest of Omaha. The eight-year-old girl, Janet Hunter, had been playing on the ninety-acre farm of her grandfather, Samuel Cross, sixty-one, and disappeared shortly before noon yesterday. When she did not return, townspeople joined state and local police in a search of the entire area which was still going on after midnight.

"Meanwhile, the missing girl's mother, Marian Hunter, who divorced her ballplayer husband two years ago, told authorities she feared the girl might have been kidnaped by enemies of her ex-husband. Hunter earlier this year managed a minor league team in New York State on which one player, Walt Corio, thirty-five, was exposed as a man who several years ago was banned from baseball for life in a gambling scandal.

"In Washington today, diplomatic envoys from ..."

Hunter turned it off. The highway stretched out straight before him. The needle of the speedometer hovered over the 80. Off the highway at intervals to either side there were dirt roads, leading in to old white farmhouses. Large trees, tired in the late summer, leaned sadly out over the highway.

One word stood out in Hunter's mind now—the word *kidnap*. He thought of Corio, and then not so much of Corio as of the girl, Jo Ann, and what she had said: *"Don't forget that Corio and I are friends.... If you think you've heard the last of me ..."*

Up ahead, there were lights—lights that swung crazily across the highway as if a railroad flagman were up there, going about his business. Hunter started braking the car as he came closer. His tires were squealing as he came to a stop just in front of the roadblock. A state trooper came over and shone his flashlight in Hunter's face.

"Fast one," the trooper said.

"I'm Stat Hunter."

"Push over," the trooper said. He got in at the wheel of the car and leaned out the window to say something to two other troopers. "This is Stat Hunter now. I'll take him in."

One of the other troopers moved the longhorse almost to the side of the road, and the car took off again. The trooper did not look at Hunter as he talked.

"Where'd you come in from?"

"St. Louis," Hunter said.

"There's no sign of her," the trooper said, "and that's a good sign. They dragged the lake and went through some old ice boxes out back of the Messings' place. Most of them are up looking in the Black Woods now. You know where that is?"

"Yes," Hunter said. "What about a kidnap?"

"Don't know," the trooper said. "Wouldn't tell you one way, wouldn't tell you another. Wouldn't be fair either way. They've got a nine-state alarm out for this Carsi-Corio and they're watching the busses and the trains and the planes. No sign of him."

"Where'd you say they were now? The people looking. In the Black Woods?"

"In and around there." The trooper shivered momentarily in the early-morning cold. It was quite light by now, but the clouds were stacked gray in the sky and there was no sunlight. "They worked that way from the house."

"Let's go there, then."

Now the trooper did look at Stat Hunter, but only for a moment. "Okay."

At the next side road he turned the rented car hard left, almost without reducing speed, and they swayed onto a narrow macadam surface. The area known as the Black Woods, a forest of almost ten square miles, seemed to be approaching them in the grayness on the right up ahead. The trooper brought the car to a stop behind other cars lined up beside a cornfield that separated the woods from the road.

"You want to go in there yourself or you want me to come with you?"

"Up to you," Hunter said. "You know more about this than I do."

The trooper thought for a moment. He was a big man with a very red face. "Hell," he said, "I'll go with you."

They walked between the rows of corn—the field was wider than Stat Hunter had imagined—and when they got to the woods, the trooper said, "I don't know what you want to do. I don't know whether they've covered this part yet or not."

"Well," Hunter said, "I suppose one way's as good as another. What do you think? Should we find the others?"

"Okay," the trooper said. They were moving more deeply into the woods now, the twigs of a dry summer cracking under their feet on the brown forest floor.

They walked for maybe twenty minutes, the trooper wig-wagging his flashlight from side to side as they walked. Great dull formations of rock showed up from time to time in the light from the policeman's torch.

"Plenty caves in here," the trooper said. "I played in them when I was a kid."

"Have they looked in all of them?"

"We got to find them first to find out. There's some noise up ahead. Wait. Listen for a minute."

There was some noise up ahead, some voices. The trooper cupped a palm to his mouth and shouted, "Halloooo!"

He did it twice more. After a bit, a light came over a ridge of rock and moss and two men came up on the ridge, looking down.

"Police," the trooper said. "I got Stat Hunter with me."

The information was relayed back by the men on the ridge, and within moments it seemed that the forest was alive with men. There were other troopers, old men, young men, some boys, farmers and townsfolk. They came clustering around Stat Hunter. None of them looked tired, though all of them were.

For a while, in the midst of the awkward phrases of encouragement and hope, Andrew Hunter said nothing. He shook a lot of hands, nodded his head, murmured a few things. Then he said, "The caves. What about them?"

"Been through some," said one of the farmers. It was old man Messing, who had the farm next to that of Marian's father. "My boy Ken says he knows the location of every cave in these woods. That what you said, Ken?"

"Think so," Ken Messing said. He was a gangling fifteen-year-old.

"We been aiming to start on the old treasure caves off back of the ridge," old man Messing said. "Don't you worry about anybody missing a cave, Stat. You come along with us."

They went up over the rocks and moss and started on a high, irregular cluster of prehistoric rock slabs that formed a series of caves and tunnels almost in the heart of the forest. There were two main caves, and Hunter went with some ten other men as they started working into them. They worked slowly, thoroughly. If there was an open space behind a deep ancient boulder, men with crowbars and tired shoulders would move to free the rock so they could see. It was morning now, but still in the caves it was dark and the flashlights finger-painted in the blackness.

"They got a generator with some lights on a truck all the way from Omaha," old man Messing said. "But it's out on the back road."

"Wouldn't do no good in here nohow," one of the others said.

They were more than an hour in the caves, and by now Stat Hunter knew they would not find Janet there. He did not think they would find her in the woods at all, nor anywhere here, nor anywhere at all. A wild, drawing sense of loss took hold of him, and he leaned against the inner wall of one of the caves, his eyes pressed against the back of his hand.

When he came back to Conway, New York, Walt Corio did not know that there was a nine-state alarm out for him. The city of Conway did not know he was in town, either. The only one who knew was the girl, Jo Ann.

Corio planned to spend the night with her. But first, he took her out to the Black Widow.

"Why?" she said to him. "Why are we going there?"

"Because we have to have money. We're going to have a talk with your friend."

"Bird? He won't give you any money."

"No?"

It was late at night when they found the man named Bird in the little room he used for an office at the Black Widow.

"Ah," Bird said, and blew his nose. "Mr. Corio. And Jo Ann. Do we have a date for Saturday night, Jo Ann?"

"Number one on the hit parade," Walt Corio said to him, "you haven't got any date with Jo Ann for Saturday night, or for any other night."

"Oh?" the man named Bird said. "And what is number two on the hit parade?"

"Ten thousand dollars," Corio said to him.

"That much?" Bird said. "My."

"Right away," Corio said. "You'll ask why, so I'll save you the trouble. Because it's worth that much to you to stay in business."

"Ah," Bird said. "You mean you would inform somewhat higher authorities than the Conway police?"

"About the downstairs," Corio said. "And you wouldn't like that at all."

"No," Bird said. "No, I wouldn't. On the other hand, you're wanted too, I believe, for—what is it?—attempted bribery?"

"Nope," Corio said. "That part never got out."

"It might."

Corio was enjoying himself. "If it does, I'm still a moving target. The Black Widow isn't."

The man named Bird looked at Jo Ann. "Well," he said, heavily. "Well, well."

Walt Corio laughed. It was the first time he had laughed in weeks. He was laughing when the door opened and the two men came in. One of them was Arnold Margolies, the sports editor of the Conway *Times*. The other man had a camera.

"I thought I recognized him coming in," Margolies said. "Get them, Andy. All of them."

Walt Corio was at the door as the flashbulb went off. The camera spilled from the photographer's hands and Corio was gone.

"All right, then," Margolies said. "Half a loaf. Just take a picture of Mr. Bird here."

"Don't you get rough, too," the photographer said to Bird.

"Mr. Margolies," Bird said, "I sit where I am and I appeal to you."

"Really?"

"I wish no publicity."

"The trouble with me," Margolies said, "is I'm mad because I blew getting Corio. When I'm mad, I'm a terrible man. I sit down and write stories about illegal gambling and all kinds of things."

Bird held up his hand, and his face bore a look of pain. "It doesn't have to come to that, does it? Why?"

"Because of the company you keep."

"Ah, yes," Bird said, and nodded to himself. "And elections are in November. I keep forgetting. Well, then. Suppose we talk it over?"

"No, thanks."

"Damn it," Bird said, and sneezed. "Damn it, damn it."

Jo Ann sat there. Her lips were parted. She said nothing.

How long Andrew Hunter stood leaning against the wall of the cave, he did not know. What he was next aware of was motion: hurried, scurrying motion, the motion of men suddenly running. There were two or three hoarse shouts outside the entrance to the cave. Then someone leaned in and said, "Hey, Stat! Stat! For God's sake come here!"

Hunter stumbled out into the daylight. He felt himself steadied by someone whose arm grasped his. Off to the left there were three rocks, angled together so they formed a tiny cave all their own. There was a group of men gathered at the opening. One of them turned and said, "Here's Stat. Let him through." They parted silently, and Andrew Hunter moved in between and bent over, looking into the opening in the rocks. Behind him, two men held their flashlights focused on the ground just inside the cave.

Stat Hunter looked down dully. What he saw first was a state trooper, half-sitting against the inner wall. The trooper was looking down.

Janet Hunter lay on the floor of the cave. She wore blue jeans and a plaid shirt, and there was a ribbon, still tied, in her hair.

The state trooper looked up at Stat Hunter, and their eyes held for a moment.

Then the trooper said, "She's asleep. She's tired out."

Andrew Hunter fell on his knees beside his daughter. The state trooper, his back wedged against the rock, stayed there in his half-crouch, red-faced, unable to move.

There were voices from outside.

"Henry's got the doc."

"Here's Doc Kline now."

"Let him through in there."

Another bustling and more action on the outside, and Stat Hunter felt hands, gently insistent, upon his shoulders. He turned and saw a tired-looking, gray little man with enormous horn-rimmed glasses.

"Doctor," the little man said. "Let me get in there with my bag, can you?"

Hunter started to get up, and as he did, Janet awoke.

She looked straight up at her father, and there was no surprise in her face. After a moment, she smiled.

"You see, Daddy?" she said. "I knew I'd find you."

"Find me?"

She nodded seriously. "I decided I was going to wait till you were in St. Louis because it was the nearest city where your team goes."

Hunter blinked, and moistened his lips.

"Omaha is four hundred and fifty-eight miles from St. Louis," Janet said, "and it's four hundred and eighty-seven miles from Chicago. That's why I waited."

The doctor leaned over her now with his stethoscope.

Somebody behind Andrew Hunter said, "There's an ambulance out back of Charley Berghoff's place."

Another voice said, "Where's that mobile unit?"

"Berghoff's is closer. They can use the phone there."

"Well, let's get going with it. Let the people know they found the little girl."

"And she's all right."

"Well, what does the doc say?"

The doctor crawled out of the cave. "Everything seems to be all right."

"They're bringing a stretcher, doc."

"You won't need a stretcher. Somebody can carry her."

"I'll carry her," Stat Hunter said. The state trooper in the cave helped Janet outside, and there Andrew Hunter picked her up in his arms and held her with his face in her hair, his face wet with tears.

They came triumphantly out of the woods that way, like a tired torchlight parade, with the crowbars and the rifles and the flashlights and the rolled-up canvas stretcher. When they got to the clearing, some of them ran up the antennae of their walkie-talkies and began to bark the news.

The red-faced trooper drove Stat Hunter's car. Hunter sat next to him in the front seat, with Janet on his lap, her arms around his neck.

The trooper switched on the radio as they drove the nine miles to the farm. They got the nine-o'clock news. The man said:

"How about it, men? Looking for success, happiness, an easy way to pay those nagging bills the wife's been after you about, a new suit of clothes and a new car so that special girl will tell you she belongs to you? Then listen carefully to an announcement from Reliable Finance, eastern Nebraska's oldest and friendliest plan to provide that extra cash—directly following the news.

"Here's a bulletin. The daughter of baseball star Andrew Hunter was found uninjured this morning in a cave in the Black Woods area near Stillwell, a town sixty-four miles northwest of Omaha. A search party headed by Hunter himself found eight-year-old Janet Hunter nearly twenty-four hours after she disappeared from the home of her grandfather, Samuel Cross, sixty-one, a Stillwell farmer. Hunter had flown to join the search from St. Louis, where he left the team

he manages, the Philadelphia Bears. Janet had set out to walk and hitchhike to St. Louis, to visit her father."

The trooper moved his hand to the volume knob and turned it down, and Stat Hunter said, "How'd they find out so fast?"

"You were nearly an hour coming out of those woods. Don't you know that?"

"It seems like it all happened five minutes ago."

"I don't know," the trooper said. "I guess maybe it would seem that way at that."

There were landmarks along the way that Stat Hunter recognized now, and there were people along the roadside to wave, and to cheer the disorderly, strung-out caravan of cars that had formed, coming back from the search to the farm. Hunter's car was neither the first nor the last in the parade, and when they turned onto the last narrow black road that ran for a mile past the place of his former father-in-law, the ballplayer could see a string of vehicles already parked up ahead, where the entrance road and the mailbox were.

The coming of Hunter was heralded by the men already there, who knew what his rented car looked like. Stat Hunter said to himself, *I haven't seen her in all those two years.*

The trooper, driving, skirted the cars that were already parked by the side of the road and brought the car around the mailbox and into the driveway.

Then he brought the car to a gentle stop, and the first person, the only person, that Stat Hunter saw was Marian. She was wearing a simple gray dress, a dress that Hunter remembered. There was nothing about her that he did not remember. He remembered everything.

He shifted the child in his arms and got out of the car. There was not far to walk.

CHAPTER SIX
THREE AND TWO

ANDREW HUNTER REJOINED THE BEARS at Philadelphia, on a Sunday. They had split three out of six in his absence, and he waited for someone to allude to the fact that he had taken all that time away from the club to conclude a mission which actually had been accomplished within twelve hours after he left. But no one said anything, except to tell him, as many of the Bears and the sports writers did, that they were happy things had turned out well at home. To a man, they called it *home*.

The Bears won five in a row for Stat, and now the Philadelphia club had a four-game swing over St. Louis in fifth place. The big thing now was that Chicago was losing. With less than two weeks to go the standings of the first division read:

	W	L	PCT.	G.B.
New York	87	57	.604	—
Boston	86	60	.589	2
Chicago	80	65	.552	7½
Philadelphia	77	67	.535	10

But it was not too hopeful a thing. All ten of Philadelphia's remaining games now were against New York and Boston—two at Boston, two against New York at New York, one more (a rained played-off) at Boston, then back to Philadelphia for three with New York and a final pair with Boston. Chicago, meanwhile, had three second-division western clubs to mess with.

They were on the train for Boston when Ollie Marcus came into Hunter's compartment. He sat down, loosened his coat and collar, and put his feet up on the seat where Hunter sat across from him.

"So," Marcus said.

"So," Stat Hunter said.

"You're proud of yourself, aren't you?"

"Yes. Shouldn't I be?"

"You ought to be damn proud. You picked up eleven games in this race in less than two months. You've got a shot at third place."

"Not the best shot in the world."

"Not the worst either. You heard about Kingman?"

"No."

"In the hospital with the flu," Marcus said, "and maybe it's pneumonia. You know what Boston did this morning?"

Hunter shook his head.

"Called up an old pal of yours from Indianapolis to take his place. Guy's been going good in the Association." Marcus put a toothpick in his mouth. "Joe Whittier."

Stat Hunter said nothing for a time. Then he asked, "They going to use him?"

"Start him, probably. They've got nobody else. What've they got to lose?"

Hunter shook his head two or three times. "Problems. Get rid of one thing and it's always something else."

"You want to talk about it?"

"What?" Hunter knew Marcus was referring to Marian, and he knew Marcus knew he knew. "I don't know, Ollie. I just don't know. I'm in love with her. I know that."

"What about Marian?"

Hunter slammed the fist of one hand into the palm of the other. "She's got a point, Ollie. She's been fairly happy, and she's been fairly peaceful. She doesn't want to go back to it the way it was, when she was married to a guy who didn't know his elbow from left field and never gave a damn one way or the other." Hunter was using his hands as he talked. "I don't think she minded it in me for her sake, but she hated the way it worked out with Janet. The time I had, I wasn't spending with my daughter."

"Well," Marcus said, "you've changed."

"Marian said she believed that. But it was a pretty emotional thing, our being together again for the first time since the divorce, and I asked her to come back with me, and she said no, she wanted to wait till the season was over because she wanted to be by herself and think about it."

"She doesn't mind the ballplayer's life the way she used to?"

"It wasn't the ballplayer's life she minded. It was the ballplayer."

"Well, then," Marcus said, "it looks good for you."

"I hope so," Hunter said. "I only hope so. The thing is, I've made promises to her before and I always wound up the same Stat Hunter. She sits down by herself now to dope it out, she can ask herself what's the use? And if she figured that way, she wouldn't come back."

"I think she'll come back," Marcus said.

"I'm only hoping," Hunter said. "I promised to leave her alone till after the season."

"Well, I haven't called one wrong this year," Marcus said.

"As they say on the sports pages," Hunter said, "you're due."

Marcus said, "Never mind. Besides, there's Janet. She left home to be with you. You know how she feels. Don't you think Marian knows it too?"

"It wasn't that way," Stat Hunter said. "I mean, it wasn't as if she liked one of us and didn't like the other, or was playing us off against each other, or anything like that. How can you explain it? Kids do that kind of thing. Some of the kids she played with were needling her about not having a father. The next thing anybody knew, she'd taken off."

Marcus shrugged and swapped his old toothpick for a new one.

"Besides," Hunter said, "you get back to the same thing. I asked Marian to come with me and she said no."

"Okay," Marcus said. "Let's talk about Boston. Today's Friday. Tonight and tomorrow at Boston. Sunday two games at New York. Monday off. Tuesday at Boston. The rest of the week in Philadelphia. Wednesday, Thursday, and Friday, New York. Saturday and Sunday, Boston. All single games. I suppose you noticed the schedule."

"What about it?"

"New York and Boston are going for the pennant and they don't play each other at all the rest of the way in. That means they aren't saving any pitchers for each other. We'll get their big men."

Hunter looked out the window, thoughtfully. "I don't see how he can take a chance on starting Whittier."

"Well, maybe they won't," Marcus said, "but it's a cinch they haven't got anybody better. Kingman was a key man for them. What was that place we just passed?"

"Bridgeport," Stat Hunter said.

"I've got to look over a kid in Bridgeport," Marcus said. "He's a lefthanded catcher. You think you've got troubles."

In batting practice that night Bill Avery, notoriously brittle and accident-prone, was struck on the ankle by a batted ball. One small bone was broken, and Andrew Hunter became the regular center fielder for the Philadelphia Bears.

It was a fact he neither welcomed nor resented. That was the way it was. He would be playing center field. On his way out there, before the game, he passed Joe Whittier and said hello, but Whittier kept looking straight ahead. Then the line-ups went up on the scoreboard and Hunter saw that Whittier was starting. *Trouble,* Stat Hunter said to himself. *Trouble, trouble, trouble.*

Hunter's pitching rotation was set in his mind now for the rest of the season: Hines tonight, Bates tomorrow. New York would have to throw a second-liner against them in one of the two games Sunday, and Hunter would use Simon North in that game and Milt Sampson in the other. Tuesday against Boston it would be Jaretski, then Hines, Bates, and Sampson against New York, and Jaretski and finally Hines again against Boston. Moses Jones would be number one in relief, Paul Lindeman number two.

Hunter moved Jesse Goodman up to second in the batting order, put himself third. McNeil and Goodman had made out and Hunter was at bat in the start of the first inning when a roar went up from the packed crowd. It was the unique sound that can only mean information on the scoreboard. Hunter looked and saw that New York had scored six runs in the top half of its first inning in the other night game in the east. That made Boston unhappier than Philadelphia, even though, to all intents and purposes, it eliminated the Bears once and for all from a mathematical shot at the pennant. One New York victory or one Philadelphia defeat would do it, and six New York runs in the first inning suggested a New York victory.

Fortified by this news, Stat Hunter flied out, and, with Hines going for his twentieth victory and pitching expertly, Boston got only one hit over the first four innings. In the fifth, the Bears scored twice—and it was the hind end of the batting order that did it. Connover, Kramer, and Hines all singled and McNeil flied deep for the pair of scores.

But in the last half of the sixth inning, Joe Whittier got his first major-league hit, a double that hit first base, bounced high over the head of Dog-face Martin, and rolled out along the right-field line. The next man grounded out, sending Whittier to third, and the next one flied to Stat Hunter a step back from his normal playing depth. Hunter took the ball with his hands up in front of him and cut loose. Never at any time did the ball exceed ten feet in height. It hit the dirt for the first time on a line between the pitcher's mound and home plate, and flew on the single bounce low and true into the mitt of Jack Connover. Connover had Whittier by eight feet and, in the collision at the plate, dropped the ball. Philadelphia's lead was down to one run now, 2 to 1. Then in the last of the seventh, with the crowd bellowing in the home team's behalf, Boston got to Hines for a walk and then a single to center that sent the front runner to third. Again there was a fly ball to Hunter in center field, this one a shorter loft on which he had to come in five or six steps. He caught the ball and saw the runner break from third. For an instant he misread the play as a bluff break, but he threw home anyway, and got the man—in a close call this time that brought the Boston manager out of the dugout in raging protest.

So Whittier had told them. Not that they did not know anyway, but they had not faced Hunter personally this season, and they might not have been certain. No, Whittier had told them. *The old man makes one good throw and his arm's dead. Run him.*

Gerald Hines pitched grimly, almost bitterly the rest of the way. Defensively, Stat Hunter still could go and get them, breaking instinctively as few outfielders could do, only Joe and Vince DiMaggio, and Henrich, and Terry Moore, and a bare handful of others in Stat Hunter's time. And in a make-or-break situation, his arm might still have a throw left. No, there was no point in Hunter's taking himself out of there. He would be in center field the rest of the way, for better or for worse.

Hines won it, 2 to 1, for his twentieth. New York had won its game, and now led Boston by three games—four in the lost column. Chicago lost, and now the Bears were only a game and a half out of third.

Saturday, Hobo Bates beat Boston 7 to 1. New York also lost. Chicago lost again, and the Bears were a half a game out of third place.

In New York Sunday, North struck out nine and still lost the opener 3 to 0, but Milt Sampson pitched an exciting one-hitter and Stat Hunter got four hits as the Bears won the second game 7 to 0. Chicago also divided, and still held third place by half a game. Boston won its game.

Everybody was off Monday. Tuesday the Bears were back in Boston for a night game, and Boston beat Jaretski 5 to 2, scoring one run and setting up another on Hunter's arm. Chicago was idle but New York was winning. Now the standings were:

	W	L	PCT.	G.B.
New York...............	90	59	.604	—
Boston.....................	88	62	.587	2½
Chicago..................	81	68	.544	9
Philadelphia...........	80	69	.537	10

New York, Chicago, and Philadelphia each had five games left to play. Boston had four.

New York came into Philadelphia, hoping to lock it up. They were scheduled for afternoon games Wednesday, Thursday, and Friday.

Stat Hunter was scheduled for something too—something he did not expect. She was waiting for him when he came down to the hotel lobby on Wednesday morning, and by the time he saw who it was it was too late for him to avoid her.

"Well," he said. "Jo Ann."

"Hello, Mr. Manager." She took his arm. "Buy my breakfast?"

"All right," he said. "Come on."

They went into the coffee shop and sat at a table along the far wall.

"Well," she said, "how do I look? Pretty as ever?"

"Beautiful," Hunter said.

"I knew you'd say that. You can say nice things when you want to, Stat."

"Yup," he said. "And what brings you to Philadelphia?"

"A man."

"Should I ask which one?"

"Do you think you have to?"

"No," he said, hopelessly, "I guess not. Did you really come all the way from Conway just for that?"

"Suppose I tell you something," she said, and he felt there was anger in her voice. "You want to know what it is? Well, I'll tell you. You ruined it for me. You got rid of Whittier and you got rid of Corio and you fixed it so your sports-writing friend blew the whistle on the Black Widow."

"I did all this?"

The waitress came with the orange juice. Jo Ann's eyes were alight. "Yes. And you know what's left for me? Bird. An old man with hay fever. And he's not even making any money any more. That's what's left for me."

"Well," Hunter said, "if it was a ballplayer you wanted, you really blew it. You should have latched onto Simon North. He's the one who's really going places."

"I grew up with him," Jo Ann said. "What about it?"

"Just the irony, that's all. He was the only local boy on the whole club, and he was the one man you overlooked."

"No." She shook her head. "You're the one who's overlooking something. There's only one I was in love with."

"Who?"

"You." She smiled. "Joe Whittier got mad when I told him. He's still mad at you because of that."

"Well," Hunter said, "there are some things I can't help." He looked at her. "And you're one of them, Jo Ann. You're wasting your time with me. I don't know how to say it any other way than just to say it. You're wasting your time. Now, that's English. Do you understand it?"

"Sure," she said. "Your wife. Your ever-loving wife."

Hunter shrugged. "Drink your orange juice."

She looked at her glass. Then, with a sudden motion, she lifted it and threw the contents in his face.

Hunter would never forget the rapidity with which the manager of the coffee shop reached their table. "Something wrong, Mr. Hunter? Anything I can do?"

Hunter blinked and brought his napkin to his face. "Yes," he said, "as a matter of fact, there is. See that this young lady gets put on a train for Conway, New York. You got that? Conway, New York. I'll settle up with you later."

Jo Ann stood up. "Just come back to Conway, Mr. Manager. Come back and ask me then if I'll be your girl. See what I say."

Hunter told himself in the clubhouse that he might well revisit Conway during the off season. Monk Gladstone had finished in second place with the Conway team and then had won the playoffs, and it was something that made Hunter feel less guilty about having left along with Whittier and North. He thought of the old caretaker at Fairchild Park, Jack Merced, and figured it had been a good season for the old man.

Now he went out onto the field and watched the Philadelphia Bears go through their pre-game practice. A few changes here, some strengthening in the catching and on the bench over the winter, and they could take a run at the pennant next year. Now the important thing was third place. The difference in the individual shares from the World Series, depending upon whether you finished fourth or third, was not immense, but the Bears had something now that they had not evidenced when Stat Hunter took over from Morrison. It was a deceptively simple something. They wanted to win. They wanted to win for a manager who liked baseball too much to let it run his life. This they had not expected.

But they were even, because the manager had not expected it either.

He felt pride within him as he watched them working out before the game. The irritations and antagonisms that he had found when he took over the team had subsided; the players were loose, and they were optimistic, too. They looked like a club that planned to win three straight from New York, which was more than optimism.

But today, Wednesday, Hines was going, and he was strong. They were hitting him, but the hits were coming with two out. The New York catcher, leading the league with a .342 batting average, tried to spoil the Philadelphia righthander in the second inning by fouling off five straight after the count had run to two-and-two.

Hines decided the hell with it. He threw the man a meat ball, and the batter rang it off the left-center field wall for a double. Then Gerald Hines struck out the next man to end the inning.

In the third inning, Philadelphia scored. With two out, McNeil and Goodman both drag-bunted, and New York messed them up one after the other. Then Stat Hunter got the pitch he wanted, a pitch he had not seen since his return to the majors. It was a screwball, a trifle high, a trifle inside. The pitcher had wanted it to break more than it did, and even then he was taking a chance.

Hunter hit it as far as he had ever hit a ball in his life. It was headed for the upper deck in left field, but as it traveled it seemed to keep rising, and it cleared the roof for a three-run homer, a shot that went at least four hundred feet.

Every last one of his players had come up onto the lip of the dugout to applaud him when he got there. The stands, more than half filled on this weekday in late September, rocked in salute.

"Stat," Lynn Watson said, "keep that up and you may be the second Mickey Mantle."

"No," Hunter said, straight-faced. "I don't bat switch." Philadelphia won the game, 5 to 1, for Hines's twenty-first. Chicago won too. Boston did not play.

The next day, it was Hobo Bates's turn. He had not done well against New York on the season, but New York was tight now. Holding first place since mid-May had built up the strain, and it was telling. They were a good club, and they figured for the pennant, but they were not going to win it this way. They might back in—percentages, and their edge in the lost column, suggested they would—but then they would not be rested for the World Series. In the other league, the pennant had been clinched a week ago.

Today, Thursday, Bates shut them out. He threw nothing but slow stuff, and New York was hitting in a smokestack all day long. Stat Hunter, in center field, had eight putouts. At bat, he had two singles, and Philadelphia got four runs in the first five innings. Hunter's arm, by now, was next to useless, but he did not have to make a play with it.

He had taken, in fielding practice before each game, to cutting loose with the best throw he had to the plate, then his best throw to third base. The action would leave his shoulder hot and tingling, but it was for advertising purposes, and Hunter had decided it was worth it. He did not know what he would do if a game actually depended upon his throw.

Bates took his shutout 6 to 0, and the next day there was a crowd of twenty-five thousand to watch the last game of the year between the teams. For one thing, Milt Sampson, the righthander who had thrown the one-hitter against New York the previous Sunday, was going today for the Bears. For another, Chicago had lost its game yesterday, and now Philadelphia was tied for third place. Boston had won its game, too, and New York's league lead was down to one game.

Sampson was throwing no one-hitters today. He got racked up in the second inning, and Hunter brought in Lindeman from the bullpen. They were three runs in the well when Lindeman got them out. The manager might have called for Moses Jones instead, but he would want Jones later in case Philadelphia got some runs and he had to use a pinch-hitter for Lindeman.

Dog-face Martin hit his thirtieth home run of the season in the fifth inning to bring it back to 3-2. In the seventh, Lindeman dropped a single back of the second baseman, and Hunter yanked him then and there, sending Don Laws in to run for him. Managing the home team, Stat Hunter was playing it for the tie. He had McNeil bunt the runner to second base. Jesse Goodman singled him home, went to second on the throw-in, and got up and made it to third when the throwback to second base caromed off the shortstop's glove.

Then Stat Hunter squeezed Goodman home with the lead run, and Moses Jones came in to pitch the eighth and ninth.

In the top of the ninth, New York's big-hitting catcher tagged Mose for a home run to tie the score, at 4-4. Hunter watched the ball clear the right field wall and thought, *That's why they're in first place.*

But with one out in the last half of the tenth inning, Dog-face Martin hit his thirty-first home run of the year. Philadelphia won it, 5 to 4, to finish a sweep of the league leaders.

In night games, Boston won and Chicago lost. Throughout the country, excited fans read the standings now:

	W	L	PCT.	G.B.
New York..........	90	62	.592	—
Boston..............	90	62	.592	—
Philadelphia.....	83	69	.546	7
Chicago............	82	70	.539	8

Tomorrow Boston would be in town.

Stat Hunter slept only a little. Early in the evening he had received a visit from Harvey Gilbert of the league office. Gilbert came right to the point.

"Stat, we want nothing but baseball tomorrow and Sunday."

"What do you think you're going to get?"

Gilbert shook his head and gestured in irritation. "You know what I mean. The way it stands now, Boston's winning its night game. They win, that means the pennant can't be decided till Sunday. If then. We're giving you Tim Nance's team." Nance was the best umpire in the league, and the three other umpires with him all were good. "Your series is more important than the series New York will be playing, because you're in third place and New York's playing a second-division club. The umpires are going to go all out to go along with you. They're not going to do any showboating on their own. But the first pitcher sticks a ball in somebody's ear, there's going to be trouble. We're telling the same thing to the other club."

"Nobody's going to throw at any heads," Hunter said.

"Who throws for you tomorrow?"

"Jaretski."

"Boston beat him Tuesday."

"I can read the papers too," Stat Hunter said. "Bates and Sampson are both tired. I can't feed them North or Geller or Matson. I've got Lindeman and Jones in my bullpen. Hines is going to go Sunday. You got any ideas?"

Gilbert shook his head. "No," he said.

"If you can come up with a better man, go ahead and pick my pitcher for me."

"I'm not trying to pick your pitcher for you."

"Okay," Hunter said. "Then it's Jaretski."

"Listen," Gilbert said, "this is my job. I don't have to tell you the rules."

"No," Hunter said, "you don't."

"Just play baseball, is all," Gilbert said, and put on his hat and left.

Tom Jaretski said he felt all right. Hunter had Dave Donald, the coach, catch his warm-up throws, and Donald said Jaretski's stuff was all right.

"How's his control?"

"Not as good as I'd like."

"Is it bad?"

"I told you, Stat. It's not good."

"He better find it pretty quick."

"I know it," Donald said.

Jaretski sat on the bench with his jacket on, and Hunter went over to him while Lynn Watson was taking out the line-up card to meet the umpires at home plate.

"Listen, Tom," Hunter said. "Do you think I am a good manager?"

"You're damn right," Jaretski said.

"Well, they told me if I made it to fourth place I'd have the club next year. So what you're worrying about is beyond me."

"I want to beat these bastards," Jaretski said.

"Okay," Hunter said, and then the bell was ringing, and over the public address system came the strains of the Bears March, and the Philadelphia team was bounding up out of the dugout— Watson and Goodman running side by side, stride for stride, till the former stopped at third base while Goodman kept going into left field; McNeil and Stat Hunter going out together, Kramer trotting by himself to second base, Kyle Smith high-stepping out along the right-field line, Dog-face Martin stopping at first base, Connover and Jaretski coming out together.

Jaretski took five throws and then Connover shot the ball down to McNeil at second base. McNeil flipped it to Steve Kramer, Kramer whipped it underhand to Martin, Martin threw it to Lynn Watson, and the third baseman went over to the mound, rubbing the ball and handing it to Jaretski.

Jaretski poised, studied, came around and delivered, and the Boston lead-off man fell sprawling away from the high inside fast ball. The big crowd bellowed, and Tim Nance, umpiring behind the plate, came striding out with his mask off, talking as he came.

It had been a slip, but there were specific orders out against a pitch like that. In center field, Stat Hunter worked the spearmint gum vigorously in his mouth. It was going to be a long game.

But nothing of further note happened until the top of the third. Then Jaretski went high and inside against another bat-ter—Joe Whittier. This time, it was no accident.

Amid an alto thunder from the stands, Stat Hunter came in at a lope from center field. Jaretski, Connover, and Nance were at the mound. Jaretski's voice was an angry, high-pitched snarl.

"You heard what that bush-league screw called me! What do you mean don't pitch him that way? I'll murder him with the next one!"

One of the things that made Tim Nance a great umpire was the set of eyes he had in the back of his head. He turned now just in time to see Whittier advancing from the plate, bat held menac-ingly in hand.

"Get back where you belong, mister," Nance said evenly, "or I'll have you thrown out of baseball." The way he said it some-how conveyed the impression that he knew every last line of Joe Whittier's background, including the money and the gamblers and the whisky and the women.

Whittier stopped where he was.

"And don't open your mouth again," Nance said.

Whittier turned around and went back to the plate.

"Now, you," Nance said to Jaretski. "I don't care what they call you. Another head ball and you're out of here. If your manager opens his mouth, he's out too. Do we understand each other?"

Jack Connover, the catcher, said, "Come on, let's play ball." Without having said anything, Hunter whacked Jaretski and went back to center field.

The noise from the crowd blended into the encouraging shouts of the Bears in the field and the furious bench jockeying from the Boston dugout. Joe Whittier hit the next pitch to left field for a single.

Jaretski kept him close. Three times he threw to Dogface Martin, and twice Whittier had to get back on his hands. Then Jaretski threw to the next man, and the hitter hung out the clothes over the head of Bob McNeil.

Stat Hunter fielded the ball with his gloved hand and saw that Whittier had made the turn at second and was digging for third. The ball left Stat Hunter's hand like a rifle shot. It drilled on the fly into Lynn Watson's glove, two inches above the ground on the infield side of third base and Whittier came sliding right into the tag. Watson had hardly moved from the time he took up position to receive the ball till the umpire called Whittier out.

Now there was one away, but the Boston pitcher singled cleanly to right field, sending the runner to third, and when the lead-off man followed with a scoring single to left, Stat Hunter waved for Moses Jones. Jaretski fumed on the mound, waiting for the relief man to get there.

Jones took over, in his own leisurely but nevertheless businesslike way. He delivered the first pitch to the next batter and was off the mound so fast that the man coming in from third base on the bunt was hung up. They ran him down, and when the man who had been on first base tried to make it to third, Connover tossed to Bob McNeil covering for the double play.

Still, it was a 1 to 0 game, and Boston's best righthander, a twenty-three game winner, was working against the Bears. It went that way to the seventh inning. Then Joe Whittier threw away Steve Kramer's ground ball. Kramer wheeled, dug for second, and beat the throw. It was a two-base error, and there was none out.

Andrew Hunter did not hesitate. If it had been that Kramer, leading off, had reached first base instead of second, then he would have had Moses Jones bat for himself and sacrifice the man to second. That way, Jones could still pitch the eighth and ninth.

But the man already was in scoring position. Hunter said, "Charley!" and Larsen stood up and went and got three bats. "Bring him in," Hunter said to him.

The Philadelphia players were at the front of the dugout; so were the Boston players, who had come off their bench back of the third-base line.

Larsen let the count go to two-and-one, and then he hit the ball deep to center field. Kramer had his hind foot on second base; on the catch he took off and was into third standing up.

Bob McNeil turned from the on-deck circle and came over to the dugout. "Bunt, Stat?"

"No, sir," Hunter said to him. "Hit the ball." The squeeze would be expected. Assuming that it worked, it would tie the score and leave the bases empty with two out. Then for the rest of the game, the Bears would have a second relief man going against Boston's top righthander. With a man only on third base now, there could be no force play. The thing was to hit away—especially with the Boston infield automatically drawn in.

McNeil went up to hit, the noise of the crowd an imploring cascade in his ears, and as he did Stat Hunter felt a hand on his shoulder. It was Moses Jones.

"Stat," he said, "I just had a vision."

Moses Jones believed in people having visions. For one thing, it was a handy way to explain the home runs that were hit off his pitching.

"What's that?" Hunter said.

"They gonna pick that man off on the first pitch."

There was no time to think about it. Hunter flashed the take sign to Dave Donald, coaching at first. Donald relayed it to Mike Schwartz at third. McNeil at the plate got it from Donald. Kramer at third got it from Schwartz. The pitch rode in high and outside for the ball one and the Boston catcher whipped the ball to third. Steve Kramer was standing right on the bag. But the catcher's throw took off. It was a full three feet over the third baseman's frantic, leaping clutch. The Boston shortstop had come over to back it up, but he had no play. Kramer was over standing up with the tying run.

Now the stands tottered and rocked with noise. McNeil grounded out, but Jesse Goodman singled out over second, and Stat Hunter moved to the plate.

He took strike one over the inside corner, then two balls, both inside. The next pitch he fouled back. He almost swung at the next one, but held back as it dipped and broke in. It was a close call, but Tim Nance, back of the plate, had it right. He called ball three.

It was the full count, and Stat Hunter preferred it that way. It meant that Goodman, a fast man, could safely break from first on the pitch. And the pitcher would have to be throwing a strike. Walking Hunter now would bring up Dog-face Martin with Goodman in scoring position.

There were three men working in the Boston bullpen, and there was a sudden tumultuous outburst from the crowd. The scoreboard said New York had scored four runs in the sixth inning to go ahead in its game, 6 to 2.

The pitch came in and Stat Hunter swung. He swung late, and the ball sliced over first base and curved foul.

Jesse Goodman turned and went back to first base. He had already rounded second.

Again the pitch, and this time Stat Hunter connected. He lined the ball over the shortstop's head. The left and center fielders were moving together and back, like the base points for the arms of an isosceles triangle. The ball struck in between them, and the center fielder, reaching desperately, grabbed it with his bare hand before it could get by him. Hunter had turned at first and was racing for second now. He would have held up, to make sure that Goodman scored before the third out was made at second, except that he knew he had the throw beaten.

He was in there ahead of the throw, and still Joe Whittier went for the tag. He brought his glove across Hunter's face in a stinging sweep. Then, just to make sure, he brought it back again the other way.

What happened then became something that Andrew Hunter never could really remember. He could remember himself wrestling in the dust with Whittier, the hard feel of Whittier's knuckles on his mouth, like a man digging a post hole there. Out of the whirl of his feelings and impressions he remembered thinking that this would give North and Lindeman time to heat up in the bullpen.

Uncertainly, he could remember being pulled away from the younger man, could remember at least two side fights that started up as the players from both sides poured, tense and cursing, onto the field.

He could remember Tim Nance, the umpire, saying, "All right. This is a big one, and I say this to you: I'm not throwing you out, either of you. I'm reporting this to league headquarters. There will be one more chance. Just one. You know me. I say just one, I mean just one. Anything that happens today, the guy that gets thrown out for it will not play tomorrow either. You have my word on that. I want everybody on this field to understand that. You ought to be out of here automatically, both of you. You've heard the way it's going to be."

Nance looked around. "Now one more thing. One minute flat to clear this field. Anybody who doesn't belong on the field and who isn't off in one minute gets thrown out and doesn't play tomorrow, and I don't care if it winds up a forfeit. Now what do you think of that?"

They cleared the field. Stat Hunter's lip was cut. He ran his tongue over the open place and led off second base. He stayed there. Dog-face Martin struck out.

The bullpen phone told Hunter that North was throwing better than Lindeman, and with only two innings to go the manager called for his young fastballer. He told Lindeman to keep working. It was foresight, but for a kind of eventuality Stat Hunter had not envisioned. Whittier was the lead-off man for Boston with Philadelphia ahead 2 to 1 in the top of the eighth, and the second pitch Simon North threw sailed straight for the batter's head.

Whittier reeled flat in the dirt and Tim Nance brooked no explanations. He threw North out of the game. When Hunter got to the mound, Nance said, "The next pitcher I throw out, you go with him. I warned you about that. I told you, Stat."

Hunter said, "All right. You're running the game. I'll never prove it to you, but my man didn't throw intentionally at him."

"No?"

"No. If he had—and I wouldn't have blamed him—he would have done it with his first throw. Why waste a pitch?"

Then Hunter handed the ball to Paul Lindeman and went back to center field.

Kyle Smith saved Lindeman with a deep running catch of Whittier's belt to right-center, but the next man doubled to the opposite corner. Lindeman got the next one on a ground ball to Lynn Watson, the runner holding, but the next man singled on a line to center field.

Hunter, coming in on the run, went up in the air to spear the first bounce and fired for the plate. The ball struck just to the side of the pitcher's mound, and desperately Stat Hunter hoped for the miracle. A sharp throw would have nailed the runner, but this one, fired with accuracy and with initial speed, lacked propulsion. Stat Hunter's eyes told him now what his shoulder had told him a moment before. There was nothing on the ball.

Jack Connover, the catcher, was waiting tensely at the plate, his mask off, his body swung to half-face the runner coming in from third, waiting to get the ball on the bounce.

He got it on the bounce—the third bounce. The runner was across before the ball got there.

The next hitter tore into the ball and put it off the right-field wall on the fly. The baserunner, who had gone to second on Stat Hunter's throw-in, scored standing up. He would not have scored from first base.

Thereby was Stat Hunter responsible for both the tying and winning runs. He had Geller finish the inning, pinch-hit Potts for him in the last of the eighth, used Matson in the ninth. Boston still won the game, 3 to 2, and with New York winning remained tied for the lead. Chicago had lost 7 to 5 to St. Louis, so the Bears still had third place by a game and could get no worse than a tie for third on the year, with the season ending tomorrow. Even then Chicago would have to win and Philadelphia would have to lose for Chicago to get the tie.

And even so, Stat Hunter was in an angry mood when he got to the clubhouse. He was angry at himself, and it was a futile kind of anger, for there was no longer anything he could do about his arm. For a moment, he entertained the wild notion of going after Whittier in the Boston clubhouse, but he failed to see what good that would do. The news would get out, and he would end up by being suspended from playing in tomorrow's game, and Stat Hunter wanted to play in that game. It would, undoubtedly, benefit the Philadelphia Bears if he did, but that was not his reason. His arm told him what the reason was. Tomorrow's would be the last major-league game he would ever play.

In the morning, he and Ollie Marcus rode out to the ball park together in a cab. The day was cloudy, and there was a damp feeling to the air, and the news was that in New York it had rained all morning and showed no signs of letting up. If New York could not play, then it would be strictly in Boston's hands: the pennant.

Marcus said, "Drop off with me for a minute at the North Station. I've got some friends coming in."

"So what do you want from me?"

"So you're in the cab with me. Take five minutes off."

"What happens if the train's late?"

"The ball game doesn't start until two o'clock this afternoon," Marcus said. "I guarantee you'll be there in time."

"I hate waiting for trains," Stat Hunter said.

"It'll give you something to worry about," Marcus said. "I'm trying to get your mind off the game. You've already got a contract for next year. You're the manager. Quit worrying. You look like you haven't slept for a week."

"That was a lousy game to lose yesterday," Hunter said. "And you know who lost it for us, don't you?"

Marcus nodded. "Lindeman. He's not a clutch pitcher."

"My throwing didn't help any."

"Somebody had to get the ball out there for you to throw it. Every time I looked up while he was pitching, somebody was hitting the hell out of the ball. We'll work on some pitchers for you between seasons."

Hunter leaned back in the seat of the taxi and took out a package of spearmint gum and put two sticks in his mouth.

Marcus looked at him. Ollie Marcus was sweating. It had been a bad summer. He said, "Did you every try toothpicks?"

"No," Hunter said. "You want a stick of gum?"

"No," Marcus said. "I prefer toothpicks."

"You know what?" Hunter said. "I'd like to win this one today about twenty to nothing."

"Let's settle for one run more than they get," Marcus said.

"I would have settled for that yesterday," the manager said.

They pulled up to the plaza outside the North Philadelphia Station, and Marcus looked at the big clock outside and said, "Christ, we're late."

"Maybe your train's late too."

"I hope so."

"Who's coming in?"

"Couple of prospects," Marcus said. "Good ones. Maybe they can help you. They've always wanted to meet a big league manager. That's why I brought you along."

"In the flesh," Stat Hunter said. "You're always sweet to the prospects, aren't you?"

"Invariably," Marcus said, and they got out of the cab and went inside to where the blackboard was. The board said the train from Pittsburgh and Chicago was fifteen minutes late.

"See?" Marcus said. "Five minutes' wait."

They went upstairs together to the overhead platforms, and Hunter said, "Why'd you come here for? This train stops at Thirtieth Street."

"I know," Marcus said, "but this way you're only five blocks from the ball park." He stopped a porter and said, "Where is car 6-B going to be in that train from Chicago?"

"Back there some place," the porter said, and Hunter and Marcus went back along the platform.

The train pulled in, long and immense, and as it slowed down Marcus found car 6-B and started loping alongside, keeping up with the open door of the car. The conductor let down his little stool, and the first person he helped off the train was Stat Hunter's daughter Janet. Marian came down the steps behind her.

"I will see to the baggage," Marcus said.

Stat Hunter realized that this was the first time in his long baseball career that he had ever chewed an entire pack of gum at once. He said to Gerald Hines in the clubhouse, "I've got some news for you. We're going to win this one."

"That's no news for me," Hines said. He looked up and grinned. "I heard you and Marcus had to go to the station this morning."

"Is there anybody on the club who doesn't know about it?"

"Not to my certain knowledge," the pitcher said.

The Bears were dressing now, going out onto the field in two's and three's. There was a bunch of newspapermen sitting in the dugout when Stat Hunter got there. Most of them were Boston writers. One of them said, "You hear the news, Stat?"

For a moment Hunter had the wild thought that they knew about it too. But he could see they were thinking of nothing but baseball. *Poor bastards,* he thought, and said, aloud, "No. What happened?"

"New York was rained out."

Hunter put his hand on the dugout ceiling and peered out at the Philadelphia sky. It was gray and threatening, but there still was no rain.

"Well," he said, "that leaves it up to us."

"It leaves it up to Boston, you mean."

"Us too," Stat Hunter said.

Another writer said, "You got your line-up ready?"

"Same line-up," Hunter said. He took a line-up card out of his pocket and went over and put it up on the side wall of the dugout just over the water cooler, fastening it to the wall with a strip of adhesive tape from a roll next to the trainer's bag. "McNeil, Goodman, Hunter, Martin, Smith, Watson, Connover, Kramer, Hines."

"You think there's going to be trouble today, Stat?"

"What kind of trouble?"

"Like yesterday."

"Not unless they start it."

You could not make brilliant conversation with newspapermen, not unless, like Stengel, you had a flair for double-talk. You could not give bright answers to stock questions. After a game, the writers would come into the clubhouse and say, "What was it like out there?" or "How did you feel out there?" or "What was the key play in the game?" This last question they would inevitably reserve for a game won by a home run with the bases loaded in the twelfth inning.

They would say to the pitcher, "What kind of a ball did you throw him?" and the pitcher would reply, "Curve." They would say to the batter, "What kind of pitch was that one he threw you?" and the batter would reply, "Fast ball." Then one man would get an exclusive interview with the plate umpire, and the plate umpire would say, "He threw him a change-up."

Always they wanted the inside story. There had to be an inside story. Once, when Cleveland had been playing Boston and Avila of Cleveland had hit a single, a double, a home run, and finally an inside-the-park homer, one of the Boston papers had pointed out the next day that—this was the inside story—Avila had committed a blunder. If he had stopped at third base on the inside-the-park homer, the paper explained, he then would have had a triple and thus would have had the honor of hitting for the cycle—single, double, triple, home run—in one game.

The inside story was what they had to have. When you went out to change pitchers, they wanted to know who said what to whom in that little conference at the mound. They wanted to know what the catcher said to the batter, and what the third-base coach said to the baserunner, and what the bullpen catcher told the manager on the phone.

Baseball men as a rule were far less articulate than the men who wrote about them, and this was such common knowledge that the writers invariably overlooked it. At that, Hunter had heard that baseball writers were the best of their kind. Football writers (Hunter had heard a football writer defined as a baseball writer with a vest) were infinitely worse, because they subscribed almost universally to the coach's standard advance belief that he can not possibly win. Hunter had gone to a football writers' luncheon in Chicago once, when Northwestern was going to play one of the independent Eastern schools on the coming Saturday, and for more than an hour he listened to scholarly expositions on why Northwestern, having played Notre Dame the previous Saturday and looking ahead to Illinois on Saturday a week, would be lucky to win. He had come away half-convinced himself. Northwestern won the game against the Eastern school 59 to 0.

And racing writers, he had heard, were worse than football writers, because they asked the most damn-fool questions of anybody except boxing writers, who were worse than racing writers. Standard question, boxing writer to winning fighter: "Did he hurt you at any time in there?" Standard question, boxing writer to losing fighter: "Well, Joe, do you want another crack at him?"

An intelligent man could not answer questions like that. He pandered along with the writers. Only occasionally—indeed, very rarely—would an athlete come out and say, "That's a stupid question."

Perhaps half the classic sports stories that had come down through the years, maybe more, were either somewhat embroidered or downright lies. Strangely, this seldom hurt the principals. It never hurt the stories.

It was a rigid art form, sports writing. Certain events were covered in certain ways, and nothing was taken more seriously. Once in a World Series game, the Associated Press's running account of the action mentioned that DiMaggio, up at bat, broke his wrists on a pitch, and a big-city paper had it on the streets with a banner line on page one: DIMAGGIO BREAKS WRISTS.

Now, on the field before the last game of the season, the sports writers applied themselves to the task at hand. One of them went up to Kyle Smith and said, "What do you think?" and Smith knew better than to reply, "About what?" because that would stamp him as uneducated and unco-operative—in short, a typical ballplayer.

To Gerald Hines, the pitcher, they said, "How do you feel?" and "How's the arm?" and to Jack Connover, the catcher, they said, "Well, boy, going to be calling those pitches in there?"

The fact that Gerald Hines, the pitcher, said that his arm felt all right; that Jack Connover, the catcher, said he expected to do the signal-calling (injecting the faint suspicion that usually somebody else called the pitches); and that Kyle Smith, the right fielder, said he figured this was going to be a big game would be flashed instantly to an eager American public. Furthermore, a sports writer who got such eminent statements on his own might well find himself in line for a raise, which was why the writers always traveled in packs. It was the same reason, Stat Hunter reflected, that accounted for the way photographers acted at track meets. They all shinnied up the same light-pole.

Now there remained only a little time before the game would begin. Marian and Janet sat in the front row of a box next to the Philadelphia dugout. Hunter went over to them and smiled and said, "Good seats?" *What a question,* he thought. *I sound like one of the writers. What were they supposed to say? "No, bad seats"?*

Marian smiled back at him. Her blue eyes were at once possessive and fond. She said, "Stat Hunter, how many pieces of gum have you got in your mouth all at once?"

He answered juicily. "Whole pack."

"Stat!" she said.

"Bawl me out," he said happily, and pushed his fist with utmost gentleness against his daughter's nose, and went back down into the dugout.

They took a home run away from him in the first inning. The Boston left fielder took it off the rim of the wall with an uncanny leap, and it had the effect of bringing Andrew Hunter back to the ball game. He said to himself, *These guys are going for six thousand bucks a man. If it was you, you might jump pretty high yourself. You'd jump too if … and why is a traffic light red? You'd be red too if you had to change in the middle of the street.*

Hines was pitching beautifully. He allowed one hit over the first four innings. The Bears were hitting Boston's pitcher, but the Boston fielders were having a day. They were making play after play. In the second inning, with bases loaded and one out, the Boston third baseman had stolen a grounder backhand along the line and converted it into a double play. The shortstop had made an improbable scoop and throw far to his left for a putout on Steve Kramer, and it seemed to Stat Hunter that every time he looked up, one of the Boston outfielders was skidding in for a belly catch or climbing one of the walls.

It was not until the sixth inning that somebody scored. Then it was Philadelphia. More accurately, it was Dogface Martin. Hunter singled and Martin crashed a home run over the right-field barrier, and the packed stands went wild.

Hines went smoothly out to pitch the seventh. Boston got a run off him, on a walk, a single to right, and a fly ball to Jesse Goodman.

Philadelphia led now 2 to 1. *One-run games,* Stat Hunter said to himself. *They ought to be outlawed.*

They came that way to the top of the ninth inning, and here Boston's lead-off man singled. Jones, Sampson, and Bates all were going in the Philadelphia bullpen. The rule said the visiting team always went for the win, the home team for the tie, but Boston was going for the tie now with everything it had. The next batter sacrificed. Hines came off the mound and fielded it well and had a potential play at second base, but he wanted one runner on, not two, and he played it safely back to first, where Steve Kramer came over to take the throw.

On the mound again, Gerald Hines took off his cap and ran the sleeve of his sweatshirt over his forehead. Then he steadied, threatened a throw to second base, and pitched to the plate. The batter was a big man, and Hines was giving him nothing. He got behind three-and-one and lost the next one to the umpire rather than put it through for the man to hit. The man walked.

Joe Whittier was up now. He hit the first ball pitched, hit it directly into the ground. It rebounded sky-high, and when

Kramer, waiting for it to come down, grabbed it and threw to first, the throw was in the dirt and wide, and Dog-face Martin made a sprawling save to prevent an advance. Whittier had it beaten anyway, and they gave him a hit.

Now bases were loaded; there was one out. Stat Hunter did not call for time. Hines still had it, and he did not want to wait between batters.

He went to the full count on the Boston hitter. It was the Boston left fielder, Haggerty, a good hitter but not too dependable in the pinch.

He had good eyes, though, Haggerty did, and he would just as soon force the tying run over by walking.

Gerald Hines gave him his fast ball, and Haggerty hit it. It came almost lazily out toward center field. Moving as the bat came around, running to his left to get under the ball, Stat Hunter gauged the play. The runner on third was waiting, ready to break on the catch.

There had been a day when Stat Hunter's arm might have got the ball to the plate in time, but this was not the day. Boston knew it.

The ball was coming down. Hunter stayed a full stride back of its declining arc, so that at the last moment he could move forward and take it coming in, his body traveling in the direction of home plate.

He could see Hines off the mound now, racing to get behind the catcher and back up the throw. The crowd, roaring like a giant waterfall, seemed suddenly very far away.

Hunter caught and threw almost in the same motion. Later, he would agree with everyone else—the sports writers included— that it was his greatest throw.

The noise of the crowd now was an impossible crescendo. Head down, the Boston runner rocketed toward the plate. He did not understand the sound the crowd made. He thought it was for him.

But Stat Hunter had thrown the ball to first base.

Too late, Joe Whittier wheeled—stunned—and dove back for the bag.

Dog-face Martin, a man who in years to come would bless the unknown angel that had kept him close to first base so he would be in position to take a throw he did not expect, caught it waist high, his hands stretched out in front of him, leaning out from the bag, just as he would take an infielder's throw. That was the double play.

First place was New York's. Third place was Philadelphia's, even though Chicago won its final game.

It was Stat Hunter that they carried joyfully to the clubhouse. He ordered two rounds of beer for his players and did not mind anything or anybody, not even the sports writer who asked him what—in his studied opinion as manager—had been the key play of the game.

They had a suite at the Bellevue-Stratford, and they had dinner sent upstairs. Andrew Hunter had a very solemn discussion, about baseball, with his daughter.

"Daddy," she said, "why did everybody stand up when nothing was happening?"

He determined, after a little questioning, that she was talking about the seventh-inning stretch. It seemed to fascinate her.

"And why," she said, "did that man fall down at the end?"

"What man?"

"I don't know what man," Janet said. "He fell down on his face."

"She means Whittier," Marian said, and smiled.

"Well," Stat Hunter said, "that particular man had been meaning to fall down on his face for a long, long time."

"Well, I wouldn't have done it in front of all those people if it had been me," Janet said.

The phone rang, and Hunter went to get it. It was Ollie Marcus. He said, "When are we going to get together to talk over next season?"

Stat Hunter said, "There is a kind of language that would answer your question, but there are ladies present."

"You didn't used to talk like that."

"I know it," Hunter said.

"Oh," Marcus said, "and one other thing. Looks like your dear friend Joe Whittier goes back to the minors for some more work. Any slob that wanders off first base on a fly ball—well, even if the Boston club wanted to keep him on, they'd have to convince the fans."

"I wish him happiness," Hunter said.

"Well, good-by, then," Marcus said. "I just don't know what else to say."

"So long," Stat Hunter said. He hung up; then, as an afterthought, he picked up the receiver again and got the switchboard. "We won't want any more calls up here tonight," he told her. He went back to the table, and Marian wanted to know who it had been on the telephone, and Hunter told her. He said, "He wanted me to get together to discuss next season."

"Oh?" Marian said.

"Yes," Hunter said. "Oh." He went around the table and kissed her, and it got to the point where it made their daughter fidget. She pulled at Hunter's sleeve.

"Daddy," she said, "you never asked me about the surprise."

"What surprise?"

"The one I wrote you about. You know."

"Oh, yes. Well, what was it?"

"A chicken," Janet said. Her eyes were large. "A real new-born live baby chick." She started matter-of-factly on her dessert. "It only lived four days."

"You don't say," her father said.

"I even let it sleep in my bed," Janet said.

Marian Hunter said, "Chickens belong with other chickens."

"You said it," Andrew Hunter said.

"Well, next time I won't do it again," Janet said. She looked at her parents with interest. "Are you going to get married?"

Hunter looked at his wife. Then he said to Janet, "Yes, ma'm."

"*Again?*" Janet said.

Her mother smiled and nodded her head.

"And then is Daddy going to go away again?"

"No," Andrew Hunter said.

"And will we live with Grandpa?"

"No," Marian said, "we're going to have a house all our own. It's going to be a house near Philadelphia where we are now, and when Daddy goes away it will only be for trips with his team and he'll always come home."

"And I'll have a dog," Janet said. "I'll have a black dog with a white spot on his head, up over, you know, where his brain is inside, and at night he can sleep on my bed but not in it so he doesn't get sick like my chick did."

"That sounds like a good program," Andrew Hunter said. "If that was all I had to worry about I'd consider myself a lucky man."

"And just what," his wife said to him, "do you have to worry about?"

Stat Hunter thought about it. "Nothing, I guess."

"Well," she said, "why don't you worry about not having anything to worry about for a while, till Janet goes to bed and the man comes to take the dinner dishes away, and then maybe you'll stop worrying altogether."

This happened.